D1332691

WHO TOLD YOU FAMILY WAS PERFECT,

Bria Twon?

WHO TOLD YOU FAMILY WAS PERFECT,

A Novel by

Eartha Gatlin

AHTRAE PUBLISHING, LLC

Who Told You Family Was Perfect, Bria Twon? Copyright © 2023 by Eartha Gatlin
Published in the United States by Ahtrae Publishing, LLC
Dallas, Texas 2023
www.therealearthagatlin.com
Cover image courtesy of Shutterstock. Cover design by Victoria Davies (Twitter: @VC_BookCovers).
Editor Chandra Sparks Splond
Print book ISBN 978-0-578-79628-4

Library of Congress Cataloging in Publication Data
Name: Gatlin, Eartha, author
Description: Dallas, Texas: Ahtrae Publishing, LLC, 2023
Identifiers: Library of Congress Control Number (LCCN): 2023914915
10 9 8 7 6 5 4 3 2 1
Printed in the United States of America

AHTRAE PUBLISHING, LLC

www.therealearthagatlin.com

Also, by Eartha Gatlin

The Chronicles of Bria Twon

Hey You, What About Me, Bria Twon?

This book is dedicated to my Momma, sleep well, Bert.

CONTENTS

"Sometimes we get so caught up striving for our dreams that we forget we're living inside of them."

—Violet (Aunt Vi of OWN's *Queen Sugar*)

WHO TOLD YOU FAMILY WAS PERFECT,

Bria Twon?

CHAPTER 1

September 2019

*F*or some reason, I'd held Fav in the highest regard. I just couldn't get enough of him. Every time we were together, I melted in his strong masculine arms. I reveled in the familiarity of his embrace. Fav's scent was an intoxicating elixir. It felt so nice to be close to him again. Lord knows it had been so long since I'd felt him inside me. It made no sense how good he felt, how in sync we were with one another. I was about to explode. We kissed, our lips teasing each other passionately. I pecked his soft lips, he reciprocated, we sucked, pecked, and lightly licked on each other's top lip, charismatically allowing our tongues to seductively meet. We were transfixed and interwoven one with the other. I was insatiable. Everything about Fav was sensual, every move was meticulous and calculated. I lovingly cradled his face, gently caressing each of his cheekbones. I amorously received his luscious tongue in my mouth as he reciprocated. Our kisses were a dance of passion, a symphony of longing, with each subtle touch *igniting a cascade of sensations. I felt a warm growing urge at the core of my being.*

With every fiber in me, I yearned for more of him and began to pull him closer to my body because I didn't want him to stop. Oh, my God, the intensity of it was driving me insane, I kneaded his butt with my fingernails. I was about to experience an impending climax of desire…

"Girl, wake your ass up. What the hell are you moaning and coo-hooing about?" said my longtime girlfriend Harmony Jones who was sitting in the middle seat next to me on British Airways Flight 58. I didn't have to see her eyes to know she was looking at me side eyed like she was trying to save me and her from the total embarrassment of both of our lives. Thank God I had an aisle seat. I hoped no one else was focused on me or heard anything.

"Girl, damn, what? Hell, are we there yet? Lawd, they sure don't make these seats comfortable enough. I haven't had any sleep. I'm so ready to get home, I don't know what to do," I said as I sat up and stretched my legs and arms out to regain my composure.

"No sleep? Puleeze. Hell, I couldn't tell, not by the way your ass has been knocked out for the past couple of hours. We were in mid-conversation, and I looked over and your ass was knocked out. I've been doing all I could to ignore them damn sounds you've been making for the last hour or so. What the hell were you dreaming about? The shit was starting to sound provocative as hell to me. It must've been awful good, that's for sure," Harmony said as she gave me one of those looks like my momma used to give me when she caught me eating Oreo cookies before dinner back in the day.

"Girl, I don't know. You know all that traditional South African food still has my insides bubbling. It must have been a nightmare. I guess I might as well go to the restroom while I have a chance," I said, half looking at Harmony and trying to straighten up at the same time.

The last thing I remembered was having my headset on listening to music. I must have fallen asleep at some point since Harmony was waking me up. I gathered I'd been having a very realistic dream. My headset must have slid down around my neck. I reached and removed it and bent to pull my travel bag from beneath the seat ahead of me to get my small pouch of personal items containing my toothbrush, toothpaste, feminine wipes, and facial wipes to freshen up during the long ride. But first I made sure to remove my small face mirror from my purse just to make sure there was no appearance of sleep on my face before I walked the aisle.

After I looked at myself and all appeared well, just to be on the safe side, I still used one of the wipes to dab around my eyes a bit, not that anyone would notice. I took the used wipe along with my pouch and kicked my carry-on bag back beneath the seat in front of me. I unfastened my seatbelt and proceeded to the restroom.

When I returned to my seat revived and refreshed, Harmony was glaring at me and acting more like Mother Teresa. She was vividly alert and ready to pick up where we'd left off—I could tell by her expression. Harmony's perceptive eyes held a subtle blend of empathy and skepticism, a silent acknowledgment that the truth wasn't entirely present in my words spoken—a look that said, "I can sense the unsaid, so keep it real with me, girl." I basically tried to ignore her at first then responded with a look of *okay, so you got me* guilt written all over my countenance.

For what seemed like days, we had been on the flight home from Cape Town International Airport, South Africa. It was September 2019. My girlfriends Harmony Jones, Connie Dunn, Sunetha "Suni" Reynolds, and I had managed to survive one of the best trips ever. The worst part of the trip was the travel to and from our destination. An eleven-day trip to Johannesburg ended up being a fifteen-day excursion. We're talking more than twenty-one hours combined by way of a couple of flights. Going, we ended up with a twelve-hour layover in London, so we decided to do a four-hour walking tour to experience notable sites such as Buckingham Palace, The Houses of Parliament, Big Ben, Westminster Abbey, Soho, and last and certainly not least, we concluded our short visit in the United Kingdom on the memorable London Eye where we had an up close and awesome three-hundred-sixty degree view of a portion of London's skyscraper on the South Bank of the Thames River.

The entire experience in London was intriguing and made us that much more curious about the city, and we wished we'd had more time there to visit. From the moment we arrived at the airport to the Heathrow Central Bus Station to make our connection to the meet our tour guide at Praed Street, in Paddington, west London, we hit the ground running. The time went quickly.

In retrospect, it was almost hard to believe we were at one time at the intersection of Piccadilly Circus roundabout—at least that's how we viewed it, a roundabout. But in reality, Piccadilly Circus is more than a roundabout. It's a whole vibe. We stood there immersed in the beauty and essence of all it encompassed. We stood for a moment while soaking it all in. We people watched and admired all the vehicles as they tarried along their way. We saw the business of all the adjoining streets and admired London from the center of Piccadilly Circus before we ventured off to London Soho. Until our visit, I'd thought Piccadilly Circus was a building. Who knew? That's why it pays to travel and experience other places firsthand. Our trip had come and gone. It had been an amazing experience, a dream come true. From London, we boarded British Airways for a twelve-hour flight to Johannesburg, and from there was our transfer from the Tambo International Airport to our hotel.

So yes, a sistah was tired, and I couldn't wait to take off my compression socks and sneakers so I could stretch my toes out, after all I'm a sandals and pedicure type of girl. I only wear these sneakers when I travel and during exercise. I was also ready to take off my confined-fitting leggings, which, by the way, were serving their purpose as we strutted from one location to the next. There was no jiggle in my wiggle, that was for sure. *Whew,* the price we ladies pay to be cute and comfortable. And not to mention the constraints of the bra. I wanted to loosen my bra—or better yet, rip that sucka off—as well. These tatas needed some freedom, too, and they were perspiring from all the hustle and bustle of the day. I was more than ready to get to the crib, light some candles, have a cold glass of Pinot Grigio, soak in a tub with some essential oils, slip into my silky soft chemise and get into my nice warm bed.

I don't care how hard I tried, I simply could not get comfortable on that long-ass plane ride; neither could I get a sound enough sleep. If it wasn't the friendly flight attendants of the skies offering us beverages, snacks, and a meal, it was someone on the inside seat needing to get out to use the restroom.

So, prior to my girl Harmony nudging me in my rib cage and abruptly awakening me from one of the best dreams imaginable, I guess I had drifted off into a deep sleep. I ignored the look on her face as innocently as I could, so I proceeded with some idle chitchat of my own.

"Have you gotten any rest? Sorry if I disturbed you. Maybe I shouldn't have taken those Zopiclone pills I got from my doctor. Suni claimed she'd heard they work so well on long flights. *Ummm,* did I mention any names?" I whispered and snickered to Harmony as I sat and adjusted my seatbelt.

"Suni and her pills. I'll stick to the wine and a thick-ass book—puts me out every time. But to your question, yeah, I guess I slept a few hours, and I was trying to read some more but could barely focus with all the sounds coming from you. And don't blame it on the traditional South African food either. I hope you took some of them feminine wipes with you and changed your damn panties when you went to that restroom," Harmony said as she chuckled.

"Girl, stop. You're crazy," I responded.

"Yeah, okay. Nah, you want somebody to be crazy. You must've been dreaming about Fav, weren't you? Never mind. Don't answer. I'm glad you got up and stretched your legs some 'cause we still got about three more hours before we land. Twelve hours nonstop is a long haul, and we promised to look out for one another to make sure we don't get deep vein thrombosis or whatever Suni said her doctor warned her about. But as for your dream, I'm not trying to get all up in your business. You can keep that. Whatever works, girl. I know I can't wait to get back to my boo, so I understand. Girl, we've been gone a long time. As a matter of fact, this is the longest I have ever been away from Jamal," Harmony said.

I continued to listen to Harmony as I replaced my items in my carry-on beneath the seat in front of me. As I got readjusted in my seat, I said to Harmony, "You know, I suppose there is a lot on my mind. I guess subconsciously I've been thinking about how I'm going to handle the situation with Fav once I get back home. It kinda makes me angry that when he gets a notion to pick up the phone and call or text me out the blue that I'm still available. But then why not? I'm the one who normalized that behavior from him from the start, so why wouldn't he believe it was okay?" I spoke softly.

"What I can't believe is how you kept that relationship from us for so long. Bri, we're your friends. You should feel like you can tell us anything. But hey, I can understand it. You're a grown woman, and we've all been there a time or two. You know I've had my fair share of men who I thought I couldn't live without. But it was you who said to me, if you no longer enjoy the ride, pull the stop request cord, and get the hell off the bus," Harmony said.

"Right. I was always good at giving advice based on my own life experiences and of which I swear by, and that's exactly where I was at when I so called myself being done with Fav. I got off that trip. The problem is, I failed to let him know that I was done and had no intentions on getting back on. So, to your point, I never discussed with y'all my relationship with Fav because it was just a thing. It wasn't—no, it isn't—that serious—a no-label type of thing. You know what I mean. It was grown folks' business and not a relationship thing, per se. And hell, I know y'all. Had I mentioned I was even remotely seeing someone, y'all would have been having all sorts of events and things for us to invite him to, and I knew it wasn't like that with me and him. It wasn't like I was going to be bringing him around to meet my crew and stuff. I can't stress it enough, so I repeat, it's not that type of thing. So, it's better left as it is, a non- factor," I said as sincerely as I could to convince both me and Harmony.

"Yeah, I get it, but it sounds like you're doing a helluva job trying to convince yourself of what it is. You don't have to convince me. I just want you to be happy. I don't mean no harm, girl, but we—and I'm sure I can speak for the other two girls—we don't give a damn about him. We care about how you feel, and I can't stress enough, we want you to be happy. That's what real sisterhood is. We're girls, girlfriends, adopted sisters, and we are here for one another, always have been," Harmony said to me.

"Hey, I know y'all are, but you know me. I don't like to go on about shit that I know is not that pressing. Everybody's got stuff they're dealing with. Anyhow, if I'd reached a point where I really started tripping, I'd have busted your damn door down for help, but I'm good, I just need to figure some stuff out," I said.

Fav was, as best as I could describe it, the object of my desire— the man I had been fulfilling my pleasure needs with on and off for the past few years or so. His birth-given name is Beaumont Jackson. I call him Fav because he is my favorite guy. I hadn't shared anything about him with my girls Harmony, Connie, or Suni because it was just something I considered as being grown folks' business. It wasn't a monogamous relationship, although I wasn't seeing anyone nor was I involved with anyone other than him. There were no commitments—again, no labels. We were as Harmony had once stated, friends with fringe benefits, but it had gotten to the point where I knew I could no longer continue in it because I felt my emotions getting in the way.

Fav and I seemed to have had an unspoken mutual understanding—or so I thought. As time went on, and when I relocated to Texas from Illinois, I figured it would eventually dwindle, and the flame would go out. I presumed he'd go his way and I would go mine—at least that's what I thought would happen. But to my surprise, I received a call from Fav just prior to leaving for my girlfriends' trip, and he finally had stated he loved me, couldn't stop thinking about me, wanted to be with me—you know, the whole nine. I always felt a certain type of way about him all along but would never admit it, not to him, God, me, or anyone for that matter. So, when he called, it kind of messed me up a bit. I hadn't expected it nor did I know how to process it all. Fast forward, so I left him hanging. I decided I'd deal with it upon my return from my excursion.

"Yeah, but what do you suppose he's up to by calling you and talking about he loves you and wants to be with you? Where is all that coming from?" Harmony asked.

"Girl, who knows? What I do know is I don't have to fall for any bait like that. Actions speak louder than words. Love is an action word. He'll have to show me. Honestly, like you said, his track record hasn't been the best. Besides, at this point, I'm not even sure if what I feel for him is love. I'll admit, we've had some memorable times, some of the best times if you know what I mean," I said and, in my mind, I was hoping my friend couldn't read the arousal and warmth I was experiencing from my dream.

Outwardly, I tried to appear as natural as I could. Oftentimes, I'd literally prayed the Lord would remove Fav from my mind. I had done so well while we journeyed to the continent of South Africa off to Johannesburg, otherwise referred to as JoBurg, Pilanesburg, and Cape Town. I guess it was true what I'd heard it said about emotions—they don't lie, and the heart wants what the heart wants because no sooner than I realized that my physical body was headed back to the States, I unconsciously morphed from sanity to insanity, playing and replaying the outcome of how I would respond to the object of my desire—Beaumont Jackson, my Fav. But the more I tried to convince myself that I didn't long for him, I felt otherwise. I craved him. I had those same old feelings of longing and desiring Fav. The closer I got back to my reality, my feelings for him were rising to the surface, creeping up to consume me.

"Yeah, well, I'm glad you said it, and I didn't. That's exactly what he thinks, and like you just said, you taught him how to treat you and your situation. So now the ball is in your court. What are you going to do about it? But then, the answer to that question depends on what you really want from him or any relationship for that matter. So, let me ask you, what are you looking for? And before you answer that question, let me say this: I get all of what you've been through, the whole being a mother at sixteen, your past failed relationships, divorce, three children with different fathers...so what? I'm your friend—in fact, we're more like sisters—so I'm not here to judge you. But as your sister/friend, I do want you to be happy, and again, you know I've told you this before, ain't nothing wrong with you. You don't have to change who you are for any man, especially not this one. I haven't met him, but from what you shared with us while we were doing our amends ceremony in South Africa, his track record hasn't exactly been impeccable.

"I've heard of being friends with fringe benefits, but isn't that a two-way street? I mean, think about all those times you were supposed to hook up and didn't because he simply didn't call or failed to show with no explanation. Then he would appear again as if his ass hadn't ghosted you like nothing ever happened and you never held him accountable. What was all that about? It begs to wonder what was really going on. All I'm saying is, if this isn't emotionally what you need or want anymore, then for your own mental stability, carefully consider what's best for you when deciding your next step with this man or if there should even be a next step at all. We're going to be there for you either way to help you through it no matter what," Harmony said.

"I know you're right, and I appreciate everything you just said. I don't know why I let that man get in my head like I do. It's like my mind is telling me one thing when I even think of him, but my body is telling me something different. I feel like the singer Kem now, please pray for me. I sure need to get over him," I said, laughing to Harmony when I said what I said only to mask the hurt and anguish I tried to cover in my heart.

"You know what it is, don't you? You're going to have to continue your sabbatical from men—and yes, sex too. Just like you said in our rite of passage ceremony back in South Africa, it's going to be a challenge, but you can do it. You've got to make sacrifices in order to get some clarity and balance, hell to get your power back," Harmony said.

"Harm, girl, now don't go getting all deep on me. I can't put all the blame on Fav. Hell, I doubt if he believes he did any wrong in our scenario, especially since we never discussed boundaries, and again, I have to stress, that's how we always did things. Hell, can I just be honest? It was damn good though, the dick I mean…but really, so I got a little lost. I was so gone and all the above, so yeah, I need to get my power back. But real talk, I do have feelings for him," I said seriously.

"Yeah, see that part right there. See, that's where the game changed. You grew feelings for someone who you were in a casual sex relationship with, so, it's like it's one-sided. Sure, he said he loved you, but his actions show otherwise. You don't say you love someone and never show them. It makes no sense. All I'm saying is you deserve so much more than that," Harmony said, and by the expression on her face, I knew what she was saying was coming from a place of love and concern for me.

I'll admit I was relieved when our conversation was interrupted by the pilot's announcement on the overhead sound system about the altitude, local time, and climate in Charlotte, North Carolina, and other particulars that indicated we were nearer to our destination. The flight attendants then walked the aisles to ensure we had no last-minute trash to discard and followed with another announcement that informed us to remain seated and buckled in. I was thinking I don't know what it is about people who are so in a hurry to get off the plane, that as soon as the plane touched down, they jumped to their feet and caused congestion in the aisles even when the doors hadn't even opened yet. But it never failed, like clockwork, passengers had begun to stand and got all up in the aisles. They were packed like sardines. People breathing, touching, and some coughing on one another. I felt bad for anyone who might be germophobic or claustrophobic. I wanted to get home, but I wasn't in that big of a hurry.

Harmony and I met up with Connie and Suni who had been seated a few rows ahead of us on the plane.

"I don't know about y'all, but if I don't find a restroom soon, I'm going to pee on myself. I should have worn a Depends," Suni said, acting like a toddler who was about to wet her pants.

"This time, I'm with you, Suni. Where's the restroom? I need to go too," Connie said.

"It can't be too far, but I'm sure it'll be packed, so I hope you ladies can hold it. Come on. Let's go," Harmony said.

"There's one. I see a sign up ahead." I pointed as I led the way, and as usual, I was the fastest walker of the group. Seemed all the girlfriends had had some sort of hip or knee surgery in their past. Knock on wood, it hadn't happened to me yet. Truth be told, I hoped it never would. As expected, the bathrooms had long lines, but the women moved in and out of the stalls like turnstiles, which was a relief. I don't care how badly I needed to go, I took precaution to squat over the toilet and not touch any handles with my bare hands. I had always been anal about touching public doorknobs and so forth, and just like my momma taught me, I was sure to wash my hands after using the toilet.

"I'm glad that restroom was nearby. Looks like quite a distance to get to baggage claim and customs. I never would have made it," Suni said as she came out of the stall and adjusted her clothes.

"Girl, why didn't you go on the plane before we landed?" I asked.

"She did. You know Suni has to use the bathroom every ten damn minutes. She's just like a running faucet," Connie said.

"Shut the hell up, Connie. I don't need to hear your mouth. Now we've had an amazing time together for the past eleven or so days, so don't you go messing it up 'cause you're about to be back home to your husband. Chad ain't going nowhere, so just be cool. You'll see him soon enough," Suni said.

"Speaking of husbands, Harm, did you let Jamal know we landed?" I asked Harmony.

"Yes, ma'am. I sure did. Thanks for the reminder though, which I didn't need," Harmony replied.

"I'm just looking out for my married sistahs, Suni, and I don't want the brothers to think we're holding their wives hostage or anything. Just kidding, girls. Don't look so snide," I said to Connie and Harmony while we waited on Suni to wash and dry her hands.

"This is not a snide look. It's a tired-ass look. Twenty-one hours and a six-hour time difference takes a toll on you. Come on, ladies. Let's all be nice and get along. We'll all be heading our separate ways soon. Anyhow, you just make sure you check in with Zach, India, and Shea. I know they're glad their momma is back in the United States. You would think they were teenagers the way they worry about you," Harmony said.

"I know, right? Yeah, I sent them a text in our group chat. They are way more dramatic than any husband would be, always trying to keep tabs on me. It's hard to believe they're all adults now, but I guess it could be worst. At least I know somebody cares about me," I said.

We had quite a distance to walk to baggage claim and customs, which was another hot mess. There were people lined up everywhere as they attempted to get through the security checks, but that was to be expected when you're traveling internationally. We barely had twelve inches before the next person. The one thing the girlfriends and I had learned about travel, period, was the virtue of patience—waiting our turn in lines and those types of things. There was no sense in getting all stressed out about the long waits. It was better to just make the best of it. Even still, as much as we understood timeliness etiquette, when our time was up with one another, we understood that as well. We loved one another dearly, and oh what a memorable time we had incurred in Gauteng, Johannesburg, Pilanesberg, and Cape Town, South Africa, from our elaborate hotel accommodations at the Marriott Hotel Melrose Arch, the fabulous Ivory Tree Game Lodge, and the incomparable Radisson RED V&A Waterfront to the guided tours to Soweto, Kliptown, Khayelitsha, Fox Street, the lunch at the Playground, the tours at the Hector Pieterson Memorial & Museum, the visit to the Mandela House, Soweto Gold, along with the tours to Constitution Hill, the shopping in the Maboneng Precinct, and all the fabulous restaurants, it had all come and gone so suddenly, and now we were back in the States, and yes, we had begun to work one another's nerves, but it was all good. I absolutely adored my girlfriends and wouldn't have traded any moment of being with them.

As we stood in the customs line, my mind drifted on more moments from our trip. My smile was a reflection of my pleasure and peace of mind as I reminisced all of what we had done the last fourteen days. And we didn't travel that far not to experience some face-your-fear moments to include a hot-air balloon ride, which encompassed one of our memorable experiences above ground level. I, for one, inhaled and exhaled and wanted to literally pinch myself. It was so surreal. The entire time I forced myself to be present and embrace the time spent, and I'm so glad I did. I learned so much about the culture and about myself. In addition to learning about myself, I learned so much about wildlife. We caught some amazing photos of some animals I'd never imagined seeing in person, like wildebeests, springboks, rhinos, and baboons. There were larger-than-life giraffes, zebras, elephants, cheetahs, and lions.

And one of the highlights of many was the cable car ride up the flat top Table Mountain in Cape Town. We were more than thirty-five hundred feet above sea level. The view was mesmerizing. Atop the mountain, we overlooked the city of Cape Town and the Atlantic Ocean. And as heart shattering as it was, I wouldn't have traded in our excursion at Robben Island for anything in the world. I thought I knew the history behind the struggles of South Africa's governmental apartheid system, but to be there firsthand and to hear the passion told from an actual previous prisoner made the whole thing more real. All of us learned so much about the struggles of not only Nelson and Winnie Mandela, but there were so many others—countless notable South African humans who were arrested and thrown in jail and prison for a lot less.

The stories told were very similar to what African Americans endured during the Civil Rights Movement here in the United States. It saddened all of us to hear of the racial injustices done to people simply due to the color of one's skin. And even more to our dismay was to learn that so much still had not changed. Yes, apartheid had ended in 1994, but as we were so often reminded by the South African people, they were free but far from liberated. In some places, the segregation was obvious. We saw thousands of shanties in townships such as Soweto, Khayelitcha, and Kliptown where some native South African people lived in underprivileged conditions. Our tour group got up close and personal with the residents in their communities and got a taste of how it felt to live amid their daily normal circumstances during load shredding.

All of that made me realize how much we take for granted in the States. We rarely had to deal with load shredding or load reduction, which is the deliberate shutdown of electric power in a part or parts of a power-distribution system, generally to prevent the failure of the entire system when the demand strains the capacity of the system. This is done throughout South Africa as a controlled option to respond to unplanned events to protect the electricity power system from a total blackout. In the States, we typically dealt with load reduction only in some extreme weather temperatures, which occurred rarely and I hadn't ever heard of such a thing.

In some townships, load shedding was the daily normal. In addition to the loading shedding, we visited some townships that didn't even have indoor plumbing or running water. Yet their communities were vibrant, and the people displayed love and care for one another while instilling the value of education and high work ethic within their family structure as if these extreme conditions didn't faze them.

As we were led by our young tour guide around a couple of the local townships amid their neighborhoods, we saw colorful graffiti-plastered tin homes displaying paintings of bright words like *I love Khayelitcha, #saveourchildren* murals of painted faces, larger-than-life pictures of South African children, heart-shaped murals painted on tin walls, beautifully painted larger-than-life giraffe paintings, we could feel the love permeating the atmosphere. Our tour guide greeted anyone she encountered as she led us through the community and introduced us to members of families who owned local business in the townships. The eloquent young lady spoke with knowledge and pride informing us about the South African culture. We were enlightened that some families of twelve or more lived in three-room shanties. It was astounding to us but very normal for them. Oftentimes, after our daily tours, we would return to our elaborate hotel rooms literally mentally drained with questions and bewildered why the locals didn't leave the townships.

But then we were questioning their way of life based on our Americanized lens. We were privileged people who couldn't wrap our minds around how they seemed so unbothered by the inconvenience, especially when we were told most of them traveled by busloads as far as an hour to two hours or more to the upper-class areas to work service jobs in the hotels, restaurants, or as curators, and so on. In our opinions, we wondered why they wouldn't want better. But the true beauty of it all, we later learned had to do with what was much deeper than what we saw on the surface. It had to do with what the people had gone through, their fight for equality and liberation, ownership of their property, education. On the surface, as an outsider, it may have looked like the South African people didn't have much, but in essence, they were wealthy in pride for their country, love, and freedom.

I snapped back to reality when I reached my turn at the customs inspector. I handed over my passport, and for a minuscule second wondered what might be going through the inspector's mind as he looked at my document then back at me, especially when clearly my hair was in faux locs and dang near down my back. All I knew was now's not the time to be judging a sistah about her crown—don't nobody got no time for that. That's what I thought in my mind 'cause I sure as hell wasn't going to say anything out of the way to this customs inspector. I guess all was well. He asked me where I was traveling from and how long I had been away, the purpose of my trip. I answered accordingly, and that was that. He handed me my passport, and I was done, I retrieved my luggage and walked through to meet up with the rest of my crew.

All but Connie had a couple hours prior to catching connecting flights to our destination, Suni from Charlotte to Chicago, Harmony to Greensboro, and me to Dallas, and if I knew my girlfriends, they like me, were ready to have some peaceful time alone to journey home.

CHAPTER 2

By mid-October I had finally gotten to a point where I had begun to feel normal again. It had seemed like it had taken me a while to get back in stride since the girlfriends and I had returned from our South African trip. I guess enduring a twenty-one-hour plane ride and six-hour time zone difference, felt like a steep price for my challenging body adjustments, reminiscent of the hardships of childbirth. During it, you swear never to endure such discomfort again. Yet, the eventual joy and fulfillment make it all worthwhile, drawing an ironic parallel to the blessed concept of motherhood, especially in a country like South Africa where human life originated from. It's no wonder South Africa is referred to as the Mother Land. *Hmmm,* how amazing. I couldn't wait to visit the Mother Land again.

I still didn't know when, but visiting South Africa again was definitely on my list of things to do and places to go once more in my lifetime. And when the next time came, my girlfriends and I had already discussed what our approach would be on our next travel abroad. We would surely do a layover again after eight hours to break up the time. Connie was the one who'd encouraged us to do that in the first place. She said we needed that break in the air flight.

Thank God we listened to her. Suni, Harmony, and I decided not to go for the gusto and fly non-stop to O.R. Tambo International Airport in Johannesburg. Like last time, it was nice to have a layover with enough time to do some sightseeing. Otherwise, our old behinds would've paid for that decision.

I thought I was too tired to even think about Fav, let alone dream about him. Funny how the body worked and didn't give in to my subconsciousness to allow him to cross my thoughts during the time I was away, and that was a good thing. It just goes to show what I can do when I focus on me and the positive things going on in my life—how I don't have time to pay attention to anything negative. Besides, I hadn't given him a definite timeframe of when I would return, much less when I'd reach out to him. I just figured if he meant what he had said about loving, missing, and wanting to be with me when we spoke prior to my trip departure, then he'd be there no matter when I contacted him. If he wasn't, then that was okay too—or so I figured. I had already convinced myself I'd be okay with it. At least that's what I thought. Like I said, I was too tired of doing things the old way. It was time I flipped the script and put what I wanted first.

Meanwhile, I took all the time I needed while I got caught up on some of my chores. I went through my mail, both physical and email, all of which I opened, read, then processed accordingly and realized I hadn't caught up with my dear friend Maysa Carr.

I'd met Maysa and her friends Isla Gray and Mona Porter shortly after I'd relocated to Texas during an outing one night at Gloria's Latin Cuisine. Even though Maysa was in her mid-forties and I'm fifty-nine, we had become close friends almost immediately. I would describe Maysa as an old soul and full of wisdom and character. In her own words, Maysa said she hadn't made the best choices in men relationships, but then again, many of us hadn't, so that struck a common thread for me. I definitely could relate, and I should be one to talk.

So, anyhow, Maysa was a caring and nurturing individual who had more mother wit than most friends who were my own age. Maysa and I often talked about the importance of putting self-first and not being a door mat and learning how say no to family and friends. Maysa was raising her teenage niece, Olivia, her brother's daughter because both the brother and Olivia's mother were irresponsible human beings as Maysa so blatantly put it. Maysa hadn't bore any biological offspring. She owned a salon housed inside a building she shared with two of her besties, Isla and Mona. She and her friends had collaborated on their business venture together, based on a one-stop shopping approach for women in local Waxahaxie, Texas.

The business began several years ago and had proven to be amazingly successful. Mona was an esthetician who owned and operated a spa salon, and Isla owned and operated a custom apparel shop. Overall, the joint businesses were referred to as Diva's. Back some time ago, Maysa had given me an opportunity that I hadn't refused, and I invested in my friend's business as a silent partner.

I had finally gotten things squared up around the house and decided to send Maysa a quick text to see if now was a good time for us to chat about what had been happening in her life and to give her some of the details about my trip.

I knew I had to be ready to talk to Maysa because when she and I got on the phone, we usually talked for hours on end. Aside from the random text messages I'd sent her with short messages to say things like *I'm in bed, I'll catch up with you soon,* just to touch base, we hadn't chitchatted in depth since my return to Dallas. It was stuff like that I knew I needed to do so Maysa wouldn't worry something might be wrong. She tended to get frantic not hearing from me or anyone she cared about for long periods of time. I called it over worrying, but Maysa said too much happens too soon for folks not to be in touch with one another. All in all, Maysa was, in my opinion, what I called good people, and I was glad to have met someone as nice and genuinely concerned as Maysa in the big state of Texas, my new home. It warmed my heart to know her. And I knew it was time for us to have a good one on one. Before I got distracted by another thing, I picked up my phone and tapped her name.

"Hey, guuuurl. You betta had called me. You know I was about to jump in my car and head ova there. I know you should be well rested up by now. I didn't want to sweat you. I figured I would give you some time to get back adjusted and thangs," Maysa said as she answered her phone. Maysa had her own vocabulary for certain words and phrases.

"Hey, girl, and how are you?" I responded.

"Oh, I'm good. I can't wait to hear all about your trip. I think it's amazing that you and your girlfriends take the time to reconnect and recharge with one another like that. I also can't wait to see your pictures," Maysa said.

"Yes, it was truly amazing, and no cliché, but the pictures don't even convey the beauty of it all. So enough about me. What's been going on with you? How's Olivia, the shop, and your girls Mona and Isla? Anything new happen while I was away? Oh, and as my mom would always ask, how's your love life? So, there's my list of questions to get us started," I replied with a chuckle.

"I guess I can answer that last question first. Ain't no love life. I am through with Mr. Todd *Jerk-kins* Jenkins. And before you get started, yes, this is it. I have absolutely had it with him this time," Maysa said convincingly.

"Girl, so tell me all about it. What happened that helped you see the light?" I asked.

"Well, you know, I've always known it would be a matter of time before I ended it. I knew the relationship wasn't working for me. I guess I just needed closure and to know once and for all what was what, you feel me?" Maysa said.

"Yeah, I do, and if it's any consolation to you, we always know when a relationship isn't working, but we prolong it for whatever reason. You're not the first woman to do that. So, go on," I probed.

"So, how about he tells me he's going on a weekend trip. I mean that's cool and all. I asked him to where, I mean just out of curiosity, not trying to get in his business or anything like that. But hell, we were supposed to be—well, at least I thought we were—exclusive. When I asked the man for details, he became unglued and said to me, 'I'm a grown-ass man. I don't answer to no one. I can do what I want.' *Hmmmm,* so I think, *No this muthafucka didn't.* Of course, I was about to read him, but instead I thought, *Red flag,* so I calmly said, 'You know what? You're right, and I'm a grown-ass woman who will not allow any man to speak to me in that tone or display that type of behavior to me by no means.' I then preceded to let him know how tired of his foolishness I had become, and I thought it best that we go our separate ways. I was sick of it, Ms. Bria. I hung up on his ass. In my opinion, there was nothing else left to say—no compromises, nothing. I had given him way too many passes. He can kiss my ass. What the hell was I thinking?" Maysa said.

"Well, sometimes it takes us a minute to get to the point of fed up. I always say when I wake up, you better watch out, so I guess you have finally woken up, girlfriend. People can tell you all day long what to do about a situation, but until you're tired of being sick and tired, you won't change anything. I'm just glad you made the right decision for yourself, and yes, what you did was the right decision," I said.

"You're damn skippy I did, and you know what? I feel a weight lifted. I don't have to put up with that shit," Maysa said.

"No, you absolutely do not. So, how's Olivia?" I asked.

"She's good. We haven't had any more issues with my cousin's husband since they finally locked his behind up. I guess it was true about him impregnating one of the girls my cousin Stephanie fostered, that dirty scum. I am so glad justice was served. But other than that, Olivia and I are getting along fine," Maysa said.

"That's good to know. I'm glad you were there to raise her since both your brother and Olivia's biological mom are unfit to do their job. God bless you for that. So now, how's business at Diva's, and what have Isla and Mona been up to?" I asked.

"Well, I'm glad you're keeping track. So, girl…Ms. Bria, I couldn't wait to talk to you. Business is good. I think we might even be going to the next level, you know, expanding our products and services. Seems all three of us are getting new clients every day. I am so glad we decided to put all of our businesses in the same building. The whole one-stop shopping idea really works for us. I mean with my hair salon, Mona's esthetics and spa, then Isla's custom apparel shop, who would have ever thunk it, as they say," Maysa said.

"Really? So, tell me more," I spoke.

Eartha Gatlin

"Yep. It's really working, and I know we're blessed. There is one component to the spa that Isla is considering adding. She is taking it up a notch, and I think you might like it. I guess it's a feature that's used at the King's Spa in Dallas. Are you familiar with that spa?" Maysa said.

"Yes. I've heard of that spa. My daughter India suggested we go there the next time she visits me. One thing India will do is find us some nice and titillating daycation things to do when she comes to town. But I was telling India the services that Isla offers are extraordinary, so what could be different at the King's Spa?" I spoke.

"You know what, I agree, unless of course you just like variety. But with that said, I think you should schedule an appointment with Isla at her spa so you get the full effect for yourself of what I mean because me just telling you about it doesn't even compare to the experience. Really, I think you're going to love it. I tried it, and I found it sensational, and since I feel like I know you and I think you're uninhibited, I believe you will find it amazing as well. So, once you get all rested up and ready, call the spa and ask for the thirty-minute vajay steam. Oh, and while you're at it, you might as well g'on 'head and get yourself scheduled for a Brazilian sugaring... Hunnnnae, you'll thank me later, girl. You'll be smooth as butter and fresher than fresh. Okay, gurl, I gotta go. My next client is here. Love ya, and I'll catch up with ya later," Maysa said.

"The thirty-minute whaaaat?" My mouth was agape in bewilderment. I was speechless.

"*Ummm,* yeah. Anyhow, girl, like I said, I gotta get off this phone. You know how we get going. We could be at it all day, and I won't be done got nothing done. You soak on what I just told you, but don't soak too long. Call the spa, and get your steam and sugaring. I'll talk to you later. Love you, girl, and I'm glad you enjoyed your trip, got much-needed rest, and all that good stuff. Good to have ya back," Maysa said.

Before I could even think straight, Maysa was off the phone. That girl was a trip. She knew she got me with that last phrase. Yeah, that was a bit much to soak on, but at the same time, my curiosity was piqued and me with my Curious George self couldn't wait to Google vagina steams to educate myself on what Maysa was talking about.

31

CHAPTER 3

I don't know why I procrastinated so much as it related to reaching out to Fav. I suppose in my mind, I had already given up on the relationship, and by the same token, he hadn't phoned or texted me since that last call he'd made before I left for South Africa. Fav seemed to have a difficult way of showing how much he loved me. After all, that was what he said, "I miss you—can't stop thinking about you. I want to be with you. I love you," blah, blah, blah. He must have been horny at the time, and when he called, he hadn't expected I'd be out the country, so whatever. I don't know, maybe he said it out of convenience. As much as I believed I loved and wanted him, I hated how he made me feel at times, especially the ambiguity of not knowing where his head was.

I respected him greatly and preferred to see him as confident rather than accepting the notion that he was a conceited individual who had been accustomed to conveniently ending our interactions. Unfortunately, that recurring pattern had been our norm, highlighting my own foolishness in our situation.

Much time had gone by in between hearing from him, and no matter what I was doing, I always made my way back to him. I'm an intelligent and established woman, successful, and not that bad looking either, so why was I hanging on a string for him? Once a month, six months, once a year, ridiculously long periods of time gone by, and still all he had to do was reach out via text, and like clockwork I'd go running back to him.

Hmmmph, so much for that. I was done, and at this point could care two damns—three for that matter. My dick-chasing days were over. In fact, as far as I was concerned, I had had enough to last me two lifetimes, so no regrets. But I knew I couldn't stop thinking about him. Every time I thought about how we kissed, it brought up old memories. I got so weak and lost all my better judgment. I wanted to call, but I knew in my heart, I had to let it go. Just when I thought I was over him, suddenly out of nowhere, I would get a yearning desire for him. I was stubborn though, real stubborn, and my pride wouldn't let me give in. I was triggered to a memory from my childhood of a time I had to kneel in the corner during class because I wouldn't tell Sister Nunzio who I had written a note to. That same stubbornness was in me. Nah, I couldn't win if I let my guard down. Nope not yet, so I decided to put off reaching out to Fav again, hoping I could buy me a little bit more time to get stronger.

The time had flown by, and November was upon me. Thanksgiving would be celebrated in the next few days. The brevity of life was a reality. Time waited on no one, with all the fuss we made about how we would celebrate the holiday like where—Texas or Illinois—what we wanted to eat, such as the traditional fanfare turkey and dressing, sweet potatoes, ham, collard greens, macaroni and cheese, cranberry sauce, corn bread, rolls, mashed potatoes, mixed crowder peas, and purple hull peas, as if that wasn't enough, someone always wanted my infamous potato salad and fruit salad. It didn't matter that we had all that food. Someone in the family always insisted we have it all. So just like that, the decision of where we would do Thanksgiving was decided. Illinois won the vote. My singular vote got outnumbered by my family, so we settled on doing the Thanksgiving holiday in Rockford, Illinois with my adult children, Zach, India, and Shea, along with Zora, my granddaughter, and India's significant other, Malcolm as the host. Our group was relatively small, except for Zach who had invited his current boo, Terry, and Shea had also brought her girlfriend, Corliss.

Traditionally, after dinner and games, we pulled names for gift exchanging at Christmas and voted to do our next family gathering in Texas to celebrate Christmas. By that time, who knew who Zach would be involved with.

Whenever I visited, India provided guest accommodations for me in a spare bedroom fit for a queen. As I lay in bed at India's, Zach ran crossed my mind. It irritated me to no end that my son had so many sporadic relationships with so many different women. But over time, I had learned to live with it. Zach was a grown man who had to deal with whatever consequences came out of the choices he made. It was his life.

India chided me, "Leave him be, Mom. It's his M.O. Zach's like the male version of J. Lo. He likes being in relationships, he just doesn't seem to like the commitment. Unlike J. Lo, longevity is not his forte, when things don't work out, he's on to the next object of his desire. Let him do his thing."

"Yeah, but I thought doing his thing was cool so long as his thing was not disrespectful to the women whom he seemed to mislead into believing he felt a certain type of way about them when in essence he didn't. See, what I knew about my son was based on my firsthand observations of his past experiences. Zach had introduced us to so many women, some of whom were very nice and intelligent young women, brought them into our family circle, and acted like he was serious about them. At least he seemed to have a certain type that he was attracted to. They all seemed to be going-somewhere-type of women whom we as a family had gotten very close to. Then out of the blue, Zach would do something seemingly so absurd and humiliating, which would eventually lead to a breakup.

As his mother, I tried to be there for him when he got in his pitiful state, knowing all along that he was the reason for the season, but he repeatedly committed the same vicious cycle over and over. As a woman in general, I found his disrespectful behavior toward women appalling. He was wrong, and I let him know it. He cheated, drank alcohol abusively, and was verbally disrespectful to some of the women he dated. It seemed the more I tried to talk to him about it, the worse he got. Of course, he acted like he heard me, like he was listening to sound reasoning, and assured me he knew better, and he'd even go as far as to say it wouldn't happen again. He appeared so sincere during our dialogue, to no avail; out of my presence, I heard it happened again and again and again.

It had gotten to the point I'd even recommended he seek mental therapy, but he wasn't having it. He insisted he didn't need it. Of course, I prayed for him, so my best recourse was to let it go and not worry, put it in the Lord's hands, biblically speaking, and hope he'd eventually get it together. I didn't know what was bothering him or how to reach him, but instinctively I believed he was suppressing something.

I remember watching a segment of *The Oprah Winfrey Show* a few years ago that featured Tyler Perry and a bunch of other men who had all at one time or another been sexually abused as children. I found the show quite compelling as well as disturbing, specifically because I knew firsthand how childhood trauma carried over into a person's adulthood. It didn't matter to me what time of day it was, whenever I felt something was not right I'd pick up my phone and call my children. I guess it's called a mother's intuition or whatever, as was the case when I felt compelled one day to phone my son in the wee hours of the morning and ask him flat out, *"Have you been sexually molested?"*

"If that's what you believe then you need to go back to what you were doing. Where is that coming from mom?" Zach responded.

"I'm just trying to understand what pain you're trying to suppress by all the drinking, the outward display of disrespect to women, and the anger. I guess I'm wondering if it's my fault. Seriously, what is going on with you? Let's talk. You'd be surprised to know that we take our childhood traumas into our adulthood. Hell, maybe it's me that you have some resentment toward. I don't know. I know I did the best I could as a teenage mother, but maybe my best wasn't enough for you," I said.

"You know what, I'm going back to sleep 'cause you trippin'," Zach said.

"No, honey, I'm not—or what if I am. You're in denial—complete denial—and as long as you stay in denial, there will be no steps to recovery or healing for that matter," I said.

"Denial about what, Mom? You want me to say I've been sexually molested or abused?" Zach asked.

"No. I mean, I asked you a question that I want an honest answer to. Something happened to you, and I want you to tell me what it was. I believe something is bothering you that leads you to the heavy drinking and all those other things. Like I said, the first step to recovery is admittance—no admittance, no recovery. You can't drink your problems away. You have to face whatever it is that's bothering you. If not me, then find someone to talk to.

Maybe you need to change your circle of friends. All I'm suggesting is you take some time to think about what I've said. Let it soak in. I'm no psychoanalyst, mental therapist, or whatever, but I know when something is bothering one of my children. I pay attention to you," I said.

"Yeah, alright. Go back to sleep, Mom. It's too early for this right now," Zach said.

"Well, know I love you. Now you go back to sleep. At least I tried. I hope you dream about what I just said," I managed to say to Zach before I hung up from that conversation.

That was one of the times I called myself having a one-on-one intervention with him.

Just thinking back on that conversation with Zach frustrated me. I felt like I hadn't gotten anywhere with him, and I had to let it go for the time being. I so looked forward to our holidays together. So, me, being the diplomatic person in our family, I wasn't about to sabotage the festivities by bringing up Zach's past indiscretions or anyone else's in the family for that matter. I had come to realize that family isn't perfect, no matter how bad I wanted it to be.

My momma, Bea, had said it to me, years and years ago, *"Who told you family was perfect, Bria Twon? You are not perfect, so what makes you think everyone is? You have got to learn to love people, especially family members, right where they are. We all make mistakes. Nobody—and I mean nobody—will be perfect, until the day they die, and even then, somebody gon' have something to say about how they were put to rest."*

That was Bea. She always had a raw and cutting edge of putting life in perspective, always said what she had to say, straight and no chaser. I will always miss my momma, and I am grateful for the memories and the Bea's pearls she left in my heart and my memory. The young folks called that type of knowledge *dropping gems* now, but that knowledge was pearls to my age group. She was one of the sweetest people I had ever known and one of the wisest.

I felt like I had better get up and start my food prep. Back in the day, I took the entire week off from work the week of Thanksgiving to prepare my meal. This year was different though, I was a guest at India and Malcolm's. They'd asked for some of my traditional dishes, so I wanted to make sure everything was picture perfect for my family, just like I used to do for years when Thanksgiving had been the meal that I sponsored. I prepared it all and paid for it all. My only requirement was that the family showed up on time at two o'clock, with big appetites and ready to eat.

But ever since I had relocated to Texas, our family traditions had changed, and I had to constantly remind myself of that. In general, my children were no longer babies and they had their own ideas about how they wanted things done, which was something I'd always seemed to struggle with. In particular, I was a guest at Malcolm's and India's, and guests don't take over in someone else's home. So, with that in mind, I decided to lay in bed a little while longer.

I reached over to the nightstand, grabbed my pair of glasses, and picked up my phone instead. I began scrolling through my social media.

"What the hell is this?"

I couldn't believe what I was reading. Seemed my son had gone off on another one of his random rants on social media again. Zach had a habit of using his platform to share his difference of opinion regarding whatever topic. I often read some of the comments just to see where it was headed, and from what I gathered from this particular occurrence, Zach had instigated a controversial argument during a debate about who was the G.O.A.T.—the greatest of all time—between Michael Jordan and LeBron James. Seemed Zach had referred to some of the commenters who were hardcore LeBron fans as being a cult of followers. Zach is an avid Bulls fan.

After I had heard about the incident, it came as no surprise to me because Zach had been an avid MJ fan since he was a teenager. I recalled the first Chicago Bulls game I took him and his best friend to. That was one the happiest moments for me as a parent just because I saw how happy it made my son. But that was when he was a kid. Who'd have thought MJ still meant that much to him?

There were so many comments, I lost time trying to read them all. I felt Zach's passion in his responses and noticed some of the folks responding were his relatives, and it wasn't anything nice. Knowing Zach like I did, he was going to be unfriending and blocking some folks with a quickness because Zach's childlike behavior was no secret in our family. We knew Zach did not play when it came to Michael Jordan and the Bulls. I just hated to see him carrying on like that on social media just because someone disagrees with his opinions about who or what team is better.

It was this type of aggressive behavior that often made me wonder what was really going on with Zach and what had caused him to act out. Everyone is entitled to their own opinions, likes, and dislikes, but to some extent, it comes a time where mature people must learn to agree to disagree and move on, not cancel one another out. I made a mental note to speak to Zach before I left for Texas. Hopefully we could find some time to have a nice mother-and-son chat. It was past time. I took a deep sigh as I thought how challenging it had been trying to raise a boy into a man.

I knew I had overcompensated materialistically for the lack-of-father presence in my son's life. The past was gone, and I couldn't make up for it, and I couldn't keep blaming myself either. I just wanted to know where my son's head was and if he was alright mentally. In a lot of ways, Zach had been spoiled as a child and was very selfish as an adult, and as his mother, I didn't want to stop trying to reach him. I had to let him know he had to be accountable for his actions. Zach was acting out, and there had to be a reason behind it, and I planned to find out what was causing his destructive behavior before things got any further out of hand.

CHAPTER 4

I must have drifted back off to sleep after reading Zach's social media debacle on my feed. The next sound I heard in the distance was faint music. From what I could make it out, it was the voice of K.C. of the group Jodeci. As I drifted from sleep to consciousness, it became clearer to me that my daughter India was up and blaring her music that loud. That girl loved Jodeci. It must have been her go-to on this morning. I guess that was one thing I passed on to all my children, the love of R & B music.

I searched for my phone to find it located underneath the pillow next to me. It read 9:17 a.m. Damn, I must have been more exhausted than I realized. I was typically an early riser—well then again, I quickly remembered, I was awake at five-ish reading social media and stuff. I decided to get on up, get a shower, and head down the hall to see what India and Malcolm were up to.

"Good morning, my love! So, what time is dinner starting?" I asked facetiously to India.

"Good morning to you, Mom, and *ummm,* look, Mom, we're on chill here okay, so have a seat, make yourself comfortable, and relax. No one has anything special to do today other than have our small family over for dinner. We're not on any timetable or agenda Mom. But since you asked, we should be ready by four-ish," India said, not even looking at me as she continued stirring whatever mixture she had in a large bowl while standing near her kitchen counter.

"*Ummm-hmm.* Well, you know, if this was my place, it would be two, and everything would've been done and ready to go, I'm just saying. I'm cool, I'mma relax, just like you said. Have you talked to Shea today?" I asked in my motherly tone with my hands on my hips.

"Yeah. I talked to her this morning. They should be here by four. Oh, and before you ask, Zach said he'd be here by that time also. So no, we're not starting at two, but everyone should be here by four, and we should be good to go. You know Malcolm is grilling that ham, and he should have put the darn thing on at nine and here it is dang near eleven and he just went out back a few seconds ago! But you know my honey, he for sure is gonna dance to the beat of his own drum. He's a great chef, but he's gonna have to work on his timeliness. I don't know how we're going to get that food truck idea going if he doesn't get better on time. Anyway, don't you tell him I say anything in that regard, otherwise I'll deny to the bitter end 'cause at the end of the day, I'm Team Malcolm all the way. We'll eat sooner or later. So, it should be good and ready by whenever then," India said, laughing and rolling her eyes.

I swear that girl had so much attitude, and I don't think she realizes it, so I ignore it because I know that's just her personality. According to her, she's been working on herself, and since she's been into all these stones and stuff, she promotes positive energy and *blah, blah, blah*. Anyhow, she says she's a much better person than what she used to be. I guess time will tell.

"I know it's early, but not too early for mimosas. There's some Prosecco in the fridge and juice. I'll make us some drinks," India said, wiping her hands on a towel and gesturing toward the fridge.

"That sounds good. It is nice to be here, and it is nice not having to do all the cooking for a change," I replied.

"I bought you some wine too. It's in the fridge, in case you'd rather have that. There's a wineglass in the freezer," India said, pointing to the refrigerator.

"Thanks. I think I'll save the wine for later, but I will have a mimosa. That sounds good. So, I wonder who Zach's bringing to dinner," I said as I watched India making the mimosas.

"Lord only knows. He always brings someone new. And I'mma tell you what, I don't appreciate him bringing those different women to our events like that 'cause we get to drinking and stuff, have lose tongues, telling our family secrets, and I don't appreciate those random chicks knowing our business like that. And at the same time, I don't feel like we should have to watch what we're saying in the confines of our private domain either. I'm just saying, Mom," India spoke as she passed me my mimosa before she resumed scurrying about in her kitchen preparing the last-minute details to our not-so-traditional Thanksgiving family meal.

"Well, he's single, so I guess that's what single men do, invite random chicks to their family events. But on second thought, I would have thought just the opposite. In my day, a guy never took a girl to meet his family unless he was serious about her. So, I guess times have changed," I said.

"Whatever. All I know is for the last few years, it's always been someone new. I don't think Zach knows anything about commitment. All he seems to want is an easy lay," India said.

"Geez, India. I beg to differ. You're awful hard on your brother. I really think it's okay to date. After all, his last long-term relationship was quite traumatic," I stressed.

"Traumatic? Traumatic for who? Lydia? 'Cause it sure as hell wasn't traumatic for Zach. He had gotten to the point where he treated her like shit. The whole relationship was a shit-show, Mother. Wake up. You're always covering for Zach. No disrespect, but in your own words, 'I beg to differ.' No wonder he's never been accountable for his actions. He gets a pass from his mother. I don't get it," India said.

"What do you mean? I'm not giving him a pass. All I'm saying is the breakup, the way things worked out between him and

Lydia...well, it was traumatic. How would you like it if someone changed the locks to where you lived and threw your clothes outside? I don't care what went on, there's a decent way to handle things. And don't get me wrong, I am not excusing bad behavior, disrespect, cheating, or whatever caused the breakup, but what I'm saying is a woman knows her man. If things had spiraled that far out of control, they both should have seen the end coming and been adult enough about it to call it quits way before it had gotten to the point where they were ready to kill each other. That way, things could have been handled a bit more amicably than they were," I said and took a sip of my mimosa.

As I drank, I was startled by India's loud *hmmmph* followed by a laugh.

"Okay. I see this is going nowhere fast. In what world should Lydia have been *amicable* about her man being in sex rooms on social media or him commenting, 'Hey, beautiful' and 'Hey, bae' on random women's posts. Sometimes women are pushed over the edge. I know I'll never say what I will or won't do, but I can honestly say I get it. He'd better be glad she changed the locks and threw the clothes out 'cause I probably would have done an Angela Bassett on his tail and burned every last piece of his belongings up. Brother or not, Zach was wrong, and you know it," India replied.

I swear I saw her side eye me before she continued to make her point.

"The thing is this: You're trying to understand something that just is, Mother! Face it, Zach is a man, and he is doing what some men do. They cheat, they screw, and screw, and screw/ They don't care. I don't believe you're acting like you're oblivious to this situation. I swear sometimes the older you get, the more oblivious you become—or is it just because it's your son we're talking about? C'mon, you know how some men are. You know it's a thing with them, they don't care," India said as she continued in her kitchen waving her hands in the air to demonstrate her frustration even more and stirring whatever she had in that bowl frantically as ever.

"I guess what I'm getting at is how does he go from one woman to the next like that? Where's the intimacy? What is he doing?" I asked as if I was confused.

India stopped what she was doing and grabbed her forehead to show her irritation with my comment, as if she had lost her patience.

"Mom, for the life of me, what do you mean, what are they doing? You know what they are doing. Like he did to Lydia, his wife, he's a cheater. Now he's screwing Terry, then he goes and screws whomever else he wants to when he wants to. Hell, I heard from Shea that he went back to some chick he'd messed around with in high school. I just didn't want to tell you, but I know all about it, and so does Shea. Mom, I know how you hate to hear us talk about one another, but I don't care, I'm telling. You know that girl Zach used to bring over to the house when we lived on the west side, the one you didn't really like? I can't remember her name, there's been so many, but Shea knows. I just remember you didn't care for her," India ranted.

"You've got to be kidding me. How damn long ago has that been? I know exactly who you're talking about. Why would he go back to somebody like that? I thought Zach said he caught that girl cheating on him, so why in the world would he even chance messing up what he has with Terry for that trifling chick?" I said, now even more irritated than before.

"Well, the better question is what is wrong with the chick for screwing this dude—my brother, your son—when she clearly knows how he is and all they've been through. She knows he hasn't changed, but she doesn't care. To me, that doesn't say too much about her. Look, Zach is my brother, but that dude is nuts. Knowing him, he'll use some lame excuse like she has pretty feet 'cause you know he's a feet person. He says it all the time. He thinks a woman with pretty feet is sexy, and it turns him on," India said, making air quotes as she spoke the words *pretty feet*.

I quenched. I was acting like I was none the wiser. I knew what India was saying had a lot of merit to it and where she was coming from, but at the same time, like India had mentioned, I didn't care for when my children talked disparagingly about one another behind the other's back. I wanted so much for them to all get along. All the while, I knew what I wanted wasn't reality at all, but rather some sort of illusion—my imaginary perfect world. At the end of the day, I only felt that way because of my own childhood traumas. I had been predisposed so much as a child, and I would do whatever I could to ensure my own children never had to go through any of what I had gone through.

Like most well-meaning parents, I envisioned my children being successful, having happy family lives, achieving their goals, and being responsible law-abiding influencers in society. And like a lot of parents I knew, I wanted more for them than what I'd had. To this day, I still had vivid memories of times when I wanted to talk to my mother about how I felt and emotions I went through. Instead, she would sometimes shut me down and lash out at me for no apparent reason. It took me years to understand her behavior was likely due to her not having the mental capacity to give me what I needed because she simply didn't know how to. I didn't know those scenarios would carry into my adult life, my interpersonal relationships, but they had. Before I sought help, anytime I was faced with confrontation, I'd shut down emotionally because I feared the reaction of others wouldn't be as expected.

I didn't know anything about triggers and boundaries. But when you know better, you do better, and all of what I learned by way of a good therapist, self-help books, and putting in the work, I have tried so desperately to raise my children differently. For most of my life, I had been a peacemaker, the diplomatic one. I hated confrontation, especially in my own family. Deep in my heart, I knew the truth. Like India said, Zach was wrong. He and I had discussed his situation so many times before. I just didn't want to weigh in on it with India. I was still a work in progress, and like my momma, Bea, used to say, "Only a mother can talk about her kids, but bet' nobody else say one negative word 'cause at the end of the day, they're still mine."

CHAPTER 5

"*Ooo,* that food was good. Nothing like a good home-cooked meal, especially Thanksgiving dinner," Zach said as he leaned back in his chair from the dinner table.

"Yes, I agree. Everything was very good, Malcolm and India. You guys outdid yourselves this year," I said, sitting at the table across from Zach.

"Well, thank you, Momma Bria. I'm glad you all enjoyed the meal. Of course, we thank you, too, for the dishes you prepared. You know Thanksgiving wouldn't be the same without your greens, potato salad, and most of all, your peas. Now, those peas are always the bomb," Malcolm said.

"Yeah, so make sure y'all eat 'til it's all gone. We're not too fond of leftovers here," India said.

"You don't have to tell me twice," Shea said.

"Girl, I don't know where you put all that food with your little self. You eat like two full two-hundred-pound men," I said, looking over to my left at Shea. Her friend Corliss was seated on the other side of Shea.

"She can definitely eat, Ms. Bria. I tell her that all the time. One of these days all that eating is going to catch up with her 'cause she don't work out. She's always asking, *What are we going to eat?* then she acts like she never gets enough. Not like me, I can look at food, and I gain ten pounds," Corliss said as she got up from the table.

"But since it's Thanksgiving, I guess I will get some more of that dressing and ham, both of 'em was *fire*," Corliss said.

"Well, help yourself, girl—to-go plates for errrrr-body," India said, waving her hand in the air.

Initially, I'd pretended not to notice that Terry, Zach's date, had been unusually quiet during our meal. But as the evening grew on, I couldn't help but notice her facial expressions. Terry was glaring at Zach. All I could think was, *If looks could kill.* I knew that look. It was the kind a woman gave a man when she was done, fed up with a man's mess, and nothing he said or did could change her mind. And even though I didn't feel it was my place to make her feel at ease, just to ease the tension, I looked over at her and asked if she needed anything. I had long been over sticking my nose in other folks' business and doing that sort of thing anymore. But my inner cordialness overruled my logic, and before my brain waves signaled my thought pattern, I heard myself say, "Terry, do you need anything, honey?"

"No, Ms. Bria. I'm good. Everything was delicious. I appreciate you asking though. Zach and I hung out kinda late last night, and I'm a bit tired is all. But no, I'm good," Terry said.

"It's okay. No need to elaborate, dear. You don't have to be quiet around us. We're just regular folk, honey. It's not a lot of us, but we try to do family Thanksgiving together. That's the one time we're all together. And, of course, Christmas too. Ever since I relocated to Texas, things have been slightly different, but for the most part, we try to be together. Speaking of, how's my granddaughter feeling? Zora, y'all haven't said too much since y'all got here either."

I spoke as I shifted my attention from Terry. I was speaking to India's twenty-two-year-old daughter Zora who had invited her boyfriend, a dark-skinned young man with dreads and a hoop earring in his nose. Unfortunately, I hadn't caught his name. Sounded like she said his name was *He*, but I couldn't be sure. and because I didn't want to be rude, I hadn't asked her to repeat it. I figured I'd never see him again anyhow, so what was the point, and what difference would it make?

Typically, that was how it had been with my granddaughter. Like Zach, they both seemed to always have a different date for our family gatherings. I'd already figured, why waste my time delving into any background of their dates. Jokingly, but real talk, my only prayer was that they weren't serial killers or affiliated with any type of extremist group. But according to Zora, and for the most part, she claimed her dates were free spirits with whom she said she connected and who *got her*, whatever the hell that meant 'cause again, I didn't ask. Also, India had vouched for him, saying he was a decent young man.

According to India, he attended Tennessee State University and was majoring in criminal justice. So, I guess I was wrong to judge a book by its cover, so to speak. But still, who knows what these young people are doing behind our backs these days? I guess I'll have to believe what they tell me about him until he proves otherwise. He just looked a little different to me is all I'm saying, with all that hair on his head and the tattoos on his arms, and the nose ring. All of it made me wonder what type of legal work he'd pursue, but oh well, I guess that wasn't my problem, so I was polite to him and minded my business.

"Hey, Mom, do you have paper? I need something to write our names on to use for the gift exchange for Christmas," Zora said to India.

"Yeah. There should be some on my desk in my office, next to my printer," India said.

"Okay, I'll go grab it," Zora said as she left the room.

"Zach, are you 'bout ready? I'm tired," Terry said to Zach, who was still seated at the dinner table.

"Nah, not yet. We just finished eating, and you heard my niece say we're about to pull names. So chill, a'ight?" Zach said.

"*Hmmmph.* That won't be necessary. Zach, I'm not partaking in that. I said I'm ready to go," Terry said, only this time a little louder.

And this time she'd gotten all our attention by the tone of her voice. Zora was just reentering the room when she noticed the vibe had shifted. She made a gesture with her eyes to her mom as if to ask what happened. I could see India shaking her head as if to say, don't ask. Then Zora carried on as if she hadn't noticed anything different. I, of course, tried to act accordingly, as did Malcolm, Shea, Corliss, and He.

Then out of the blue, India said, "Y'all can go ahead and leave, Zach. I'll pull your name, no worries."

"Nah. She can wait. I'll pull my own damn name. I'm a grown-ass man," Zach said to India.

"Look, man, you're not about to mess up our holiday. Now g'on and take your ass on home or wherever you're going. I don't know, but y'all ass is leaving here. Now, don't let me get started. I'm trying to be nice in front of your girl here, but you're pushing me," India said.

By this time, Terry had cut her eyes at Zach, and all I could see was that all hell was about to break lose really fast, so I intervened. I jumped up from my seat.

"Zach, come here." I maneuvered my way to Zach and ushered him by the arm out of the dining area into the living room before he said a word to India and before Terry knocked the hell out of him.

"So, look, I don't know what's going on with you and your date, but I can tell there's trouble in paradise, and one thing you're not going to do is be disrespectful to me, India, Malcolm, and to this family by bringing that drama up in here. Hell, you're already beyond being disrespectful to your date, all of which makes us feel uncomfortable. You owe us an apology, and you need to leave and take care of your business. We're here to celebrate the holiday in peace and harmony. At this point, I think you both should leave," I said.

"She's just trippin' because—"

"Hey, I don't need to know your business. No explanations needed. This is not the time nor the place. Take her home and come back if you want, but the drama has to go. Just leave," I said.

"Damn. My food hasn't even digested yet," Zach said, rubbing his belly.

"Whatever. The last thing I need right now is for you and India to be getting into it 'cause you already know she goes from zero to ten in less than a New York minute. So, please just go," I said and walked back to join the others in the dining room.

"So, bro, I made y'all some to-go plates. Don't worry. There's enough food to last you a while. And like I said, I'll pull your name. Thanks for coming. Here are your coats. It was a blast. Nice meeting you, Terry. Take care. Maybe we'll see you again. If not, well, *ummm*, yeah, it was nice meeting you," India said.

"Yeah. Nice meeting you all as well, and the dinner and everything was very nice. Thank you for having me," Terry said.

"Yeah. It's always a good time, man," said Malcolm who was now standing near India as he shook Zach's hand and pulled him into a man hug.

The rest of us said our cordial goodbyes, and Zach and Terry were out the door.

"See what I mean? Zach is always bringing these random people to our family functions, and then there's drama," India said.

"It's okay, babe. No family's perfect. What would the holiday be without a little drama?" Malcolm said.

"No, it's not okay. Then Zach was disrespectful as he typically is, putting us all in an uncomfortable situation. Something was off with them from the start. I could feel it," India said.

"Well, there's no telling what it was. Lord only knows with Zach. I know my son. I have to agree with you, India. It definitely was uncomfortable," I said.

"Yeah, definitely was. Whatever happened must have had something to do with Zach's jacked-up eye and that scratch on his neck," Shea said out of nowhere.

We all stopped what we were doing and looked over at Shea like we'd all just seen a ghost.

"Well, don't look at me like that. Y'all should have been paying more attention to Zach. The dude had a swollen eye. I was sitting right next to him, and plus, I see him all the time, so I know when something's different with him 'cause unlike y'all, I pay attention to my brother. Ol' girl must've clocked his tail. I'll bet she caught him off guard while he'd been drinking. Y'all know how inebriated he tends to get," Shea said.

"I never pay that close attention to him, aside from the fact that his head is already big and he'd better do something about all that daggone weight before he keels over. Besides, if she did hit him, I'm sure he deserved that and more," India said.

"India, be careful how you speak about your brother, he is a bit overweight, but that's nothing to be judgmental about, and talking about his weight issues won't help him overcome it. Oh brother, what next? Zach is too old for this mess. Girl, carry on with writing the names down and putting 'em in something so we can pull before I lose the spirit of the season. Damn, what next?" I said, rolling my eyes and shaking my head.

Who Told You Family Was Perfect, Bria Twon?

CHAPTER 6

Family was everything to me. Even along with the drama, I was glad to have had the opportunity to spend the Thanksgiving holiday with my children, but Lord knows I was glad to be on my plane back to Texas. I couldn't wait to get back to my sanctuary, my peace and quiet.

As soon as I landed, my phone vibrations started going off. The first notification was a text from India asking me to let her know when I landed, then there was a text from Maysa asking me if I *had* landed and how my trip was and telling me to call her when I got settled. Maysa was such an old woman. I appreciated her concern so much. It was nice to have someone looking out for me in Texas. It warmed my heart so much to know someone cared, and I had learned to embrace it. The third notification was a text from Fav.

It read, *Hey you. Where are you? Give me a call.* I did that lip trill thing I do with my lips. It was always something I'd do when I was annoyed with something or someone. Specifically, this time in my mind meant, *Oh brother!!*

Wow. I hadn't heard from him in Lord only knows when. He seemed to have had the best if not worst timing ever, and I thought, he had some audacity, and it was more at an all-time high. I looked at his text and thought, *Where am I?* Hmmmph, *you don't know if I'm dead or alive, and you text out the sky and want to know where I'm at?* I didn't reply with my first thought.

"Oh, okay, I'll get to you later. Right now I'm not ready to deal with this," I spoke out loud, shaking my head and still looking at the text.

Instead, I decided to reply to India first because she, too, was a worrier and acted like she was my momma instead of me being hers.

Once again, I put Fav off. But evidently, he never cared. I didn't know he was and had always been so ambiguous, and I wasn't in the mood to try to figure him out or what his true intentions were out right now. If I meant anything to him, he'd text again. If not, oh well. I was at that point with him. I guess in some ways, I was getting stronger because compared to how I used to react to his out-of-the-blue messages, I'd get all giddy and carry on, but I was growing tired. I needed more. I needed him to really show me how he felt. Talk is cheap, and love is an action word. Anyhow, I'd made up my mind, I back pocketed getting back with him for now.

I sent India a short text—*Landed*—and immediately received a thumbs-up notification that she had liked my text. Afterward, I was able to descend the plane. I headed to baggage check to retrieve my bag and then proceeded out the doors to be picked up by my Alto driver to take me home. Flying had become so convenient for me these days, especially with the new Alto rideshare service. It almost made me feel like I was royalty or something. That was one of the perks of being friends with Maysa. She had hooked me up with the luxury rideshare app by way of a close friend of hers who not long ago had become an assistant manager of the company. And I must say, the experience had proven to be infallible to say the least.

And might I add, my driver was quite handsome. He looked to be about mid-fifties with silver-gray hair and a nice beard, along with a caramel skin tone. He was very attractive, and to make matters worse, he was very attentive to me. But then again, was he being exceptionally attentive to me specifically or was he simply doing his job? After all, I was a paying customer, and he was hired to pick me up, and one of the perks of choosing Alto rideshare was they promoted being a white-glove type service that allegedly promised your ride experience would be set apart from the other companies.

I had to laugh at myself because I was always low-key scoping potential date prospects. I could be anywhere—the grocery store, church, out to dinner, walking through the mall, or in this case, at the airport—no place was off limits. I lived by the slogan, *I stay ready, so I don't have to get ready.* For starters, my phase one, I would check out a man's shoes first. It didn't matter if he was casually dressed or dressed in formal attire, I started with his feet, then I checked out his overall appearance from head to toe and vice versa, toe to head. If his shoes were dirty, that was an automatic no for me. If his hair was unkempt, that was a hard no. If his attire was unkempt and he looked like he smelled, that was a hard no. If his facial hairs were messy, another hard no. This was just my own initial screening process. I knew there was more to getting to know a person than those things, but for me, those were some of the things I used as my starting points and whether I would even consider making eye contact. And to be honest, no one had come close to passing my initial screening process, except for the random guys I happened to run across who were already taken, and those were territories I was not interested in crossing. I'd decided long ago that I wasn't making excuses for it either. Men did this sort of thing all the time so why shouldn't women too? I was tired of settling, so I made a mental list, and I was sticking to it.

Phase two of my list was a deeper level and came into play only when the prospect passed the initial screening phase. Some of the things on my second phase were next-level items, such as religious beliefs, political acumen, integrity, character, honesty, consistency, sense of humor, and hell, even how he treated his mother, his family, whether he had been married, any children, his goals. At my age, I had a lot of things to consider, so I factored quite a bit about what I wanted and who I wanted in my life. For me, that was just the way it was, which was why I just couldn't understand why I allowed Fav to pine for so long in my heart. I simply couldn't get it, especially when I thought I had tried so hard to be over him.

CHAPTER 7

December 2019, I was at Isla Gray's place called Diva's Custom-Made Apparels shopping for something snazzy and authentic to wear to my sixtieth birthday dinner party for the end of February 2020. While there, I overheard a conversation between Isla and one of her clients as she was finishing up the lady's order.

"Hey, Miss Emma, how are you feeling today? I'm glad your appointment went well. I was worried when you called and had to cancel your fitting. You look good," Isla said.

I was sitting in the lounge scrolling through my social media feed as I was waiting for Isla to do my fitting next and trying not to listen in on their conversation.

"Yeah. I'm much better now, girl. I wasn't feeling good at all when I called you last week and rescheduled, but I went ahead and saw my doctor for my regular checkup, and while I was at his office, he recommended I order a box of N95 masks. As a matter of fact, he said, it would be in all our best interest to get prepared for this coronavirus that has been running rampant over in China. Have you heard about it yet, Isla?" the customer asked.

"No, I don't believe I have. What are you talking about? Is it something they think might come to the United States?" Isla asked.

"Well, according to my doctor, it is. In fact, he said, it's not a question of if. It's a matter of when it gets here. Girl, you had better start listening and watching the news. That's all they have been talking about," the customer said.

"I've been putting in so many hours here that I barely listen to the news. I be so exhausted after a full day here, and it's all I can do to make it home and do what I need to do there before I get in bed. And when I do turn on the television, I generally fall asleep, and it ends up watching me. Have you heard anything about it, Ms. Bria?" Isla asked, directing her attention to me.

"Nothing that I've paid attention to. *Hmmmph.* That's interesting. Let's see what Google has to say about it," I said as I peered at my phone and searched. "So, it says something about they're monitoring an outbreak in China from some place named Wuhan, but it doesn't say they know much about it yet. I wonder if it's another type of flu virus or something," I said.

"I don't know, but like I said, my doctor seems to believe it will spread to the United States, and sooner than later. And he also said it has affected a lot of people in China and has caused one death so far, so all I'm saying is we better take heed, girl," the customer said.

"I guess you're right. If it ain't one thing, it's another," I said as I continued to wait my turn after Isla finished up with her customer.

That's all I needed to hear. I was never one big on news, politics, and the like, and all my girlfriends knew that about me. In fact, once my friend Connie had said to me, "Bria, you're gonna be that one person that we are going to have to look for in the rubbish because your ass is not going to know what hit you from all the trauma going on in the world because you refuse to listen to the frickin' news."

I found my friends' comments both comical and jarring, but I realized she was right. And as a matter of fact, this wasn't the first time Connie had said something like this to me. So, after I let her words process and soak in, then I decided to do something about my lack of awareness of current news. Unlike my friend Harmony, I didn't keep my TV on CNN twenty-four seven, but I did start tuning in to *The View* more frequently. Hell, I thought, I had to start somewhere.

CHAPTER 8

It was the beginning of February 2020. I was scheduled to go to Diva's for my final fitting by Isla, and if all was a go, I'd be able to pick my dress up in a week and then I'd be all set for my sixtieth birthday celebration, which was being held the last weekend of February. As usual, Isla hooked me up with a fabulous dress for my event.

I've always liked any opportunity to dress up and wear makeup, especially since I had retired because as my routine would have it, there had been few occasions when I got dressed to the nines anymore. My attire for the most part was casual wear and very little makeup. In fact, the only thing I did do on the regular was get my faux locs redone, facials, brows, and other facial hairs removed every couple of weeks or so. Oh, and of course I still got my nails done and pedicures.

My girl Harmony always teased me by saying my ass was high maintenance. I don't consider myself high maintenance though, but I do believe in self-care, and with age, my natural beauty has become very critical to me, especially because I'm a single soon-to-be sixty-year-old black female. India is a lot like me. She prides herself on self-care and enjoys getting dressed up as well. So, we had a lot in common in that regard. Matter of fact, both my girls, India and Shea, loved fashion and looked forward to assisting me when it came time to picking and choosing my attire for main events. The only thing was Shea was more of a sneaker head, so she was the one who kept my sneaker game on point. India was more my girly girl and kept me looking fresh as she put it, so I didn't look too fuddy dud. I guess she meant outdated.

Anyhow, I was looking forward to an evening of pre-celebrating together with Shea and India. It was always a good time with my girls. I was excited, happy, and looking very forward to having my family with me in Texas. I didn't want to rush my life away, but I couldn't wait for the weeks to pass so we'd all be together again.

India, Malcolm, and Zora had flown in together on the same flight and had arranged to meet up with Shea, who had flown in on a different flight, at the airport. My one and only son, Zach, had insisted on driving his brand-new GMC Yukon Denali to Texas from Illinois. India said she didn't know why he didn't get his ass on a plane. Shea said he just wanted to showboat and that his vehicle reminded her of one of the secret service vehicles driven for the president. Zach said he had a few days to spare from his gig, so for comfort and ease, he'd rather drive his own vehicle. And he'd said besides that, he was bringing Samantha who was now his new live-in girlfriend.

We all knew she must have been the one who loved driving because Zach had never been good to drive in major cities on freeways, interstates, or any highways of the sort. It was his business, so whatever worked for them was okay by me. Of course, I wanted them to be safe and prayed for the best. We weren't surprised that Zach wasn't still with Terry after what had happened on Thanksgiving, but again, that was none of my business, and I had learned how to stay in my lane where my adult children's relationships were concerned. It made my life and theirs much easier. Besides, like most things in life, I found when you leave things alone, the situation typically had a way of working itself out in time.

Making an issue of Zach driving fourteen hours was a moot point to me, and I certainly was not going to stress out about it. That was on him. On the other hand, maybe a long road trip would be good for Zach and this new girlfriend Samantha. At least I hoped so. If nothing else, it could make or break their relationship. But if living together hadn't already done that, then what else did they need? Funny, some folks love drama and are addicted to pain and don't even know it.

Besides, it didn't matter to me how they traveled. My concern was always safe travels first, and I wanted them to be comfortable. The last time we were all together was Thanksgiving in Illinois. Our plan had been to do Christmas together in Texas before I realized my milestone birthday was coming up, which would be here soon, so I suggested everyone save their resources and come then instead. We also decided to forego our traditional Christmas gift exchange and that sort of thing.

Unlike how we'd spent Thanksgiving, we redefined our Christmas tradition by embracing a novel approach and created new memories by using a social media video call app to chat with one another on Christmas morning. Then later in the day, I ended up over at Maysa's place for their family dinner, so it was all good. By using the video call app, it kind of made it feel a little bit more personable. I could look at my kids' faces and was relieved to see everyone was alive and well. Zach, India, and Shea were each doing their own things as well and were joking about how they were going to get turnt up when we all saw one another for my birthday celebration in February, so all in all, the call was a highlight for me.

One thing was for sure: There was no cliché in the phrase *Time waits on no one.* It seemed before I knew it, a couple months had passed. We were in a new year, and there we were, all about to be all together again.

It still seemed unreal to be saying 2020. I remember back in 1999, when the world thought everything was going to shut down in year 2000 or Y2K as it was notoriously referred to then.

But just like anything else, we all lived through it, and all that hoopla seemed to be for nothing. That I know of, there hadn't been any major computer glitches, no food shortages, no electrical outages, and most importantly no apocalypse. Just to think, all that panic and not much happened at all. It was 2020, twenty years later, in February, and we were about to embark upon a very public and memorable celebration, my birthday. This was going to be a sensational evening at Monarch in downtown Dallas. India had asked me to choose the venue and to let her make all the arrangements from there.

As I was getting dressed, a random thought crossed my mind about a guy I had dated back in the day. I'm not sure what triggers some memories of the past. I could be folding clothes or doing any other odd chore, and out of the blue, a thought from my past would come out of nowhere. It could have something to do with me reflecting on where I was at this stage in my life, the thought of not being in a relationship, things like that. It's like I fantasied occasionally about how differently my life would have been like had things worked out with this person or that person. This time, I happened to think about a guy I had dated named Alli Allure.

In my opinion, Alli was a nice enough guy. If nothing else, he was a good date, the kind of guy who didn't mind paying for dinner and a movie. He was ambitious, intelligent, and career oriented, and he dressed nice and smelled good. I dated him in between Stetson, India's father, and prior to marrying Rat, Shea's father. I was very fond of him, and we seemed to have a good time together. But in life, as fate or destiny would have it or whatever, timing was everything. What had happened in this scenario was I had just gotten out of a relationship and wasn't quite sure about being involved with anyone so soon after my breakup with

Stetson. After explaining all that to Alli, we mutually decided to keep things between us non-committal and casual. And in retrospect, for me, that was a damn good call because as time went on, I learned Alli was seeing someone else the entire time.

Like my mother used to say, what's done in the dark will come to the light. It wasn't like he had anything to hide. I mean, all he had to do was be honest. Anyway, I just found it odd that he hadn't been upfront about it. But then again, I had seen signs of his shadiness, and I hadn't come out and asked him about it either. The lesson I learned from that relationship was never fill in the blanks. It just doesn't work. It's better to have the crucial conversations with a person and find out what there is to know about the situation rather than to create a made-up narrative based on assumptions. In hindsight, I guess I was reminiscing about Alli because occasionally my mind would drift back to how carefree I used to be. If I had to be honest with myself, Alli was no more than a dick call. It was no different than what men called booty calls. Real talk, in essence, us women had them too. We did the same thing, men thought they were using us. Hell, we used them too. Back then, I thought it was cool—no harm, no foul, no one got hurt, at least not that I knew of. We simply hooked up as two grown people would to handle business so to speak and be on our way. Then about the 1980s, AIDS came along and changed all that sleeping around stuff. I don't know about anybody else, but that certainly changed the game for me.

Today, I find myself repulsed by the mere thought of a random dick call, especially if I suspected the dick was entertaining another woman's vagina. As an old friend used to say, that dog just don't hunt with me. That's why it boggles my mind when I hear Zach sleeping around and cheating on Terry like he does. It's just not safe, nor in my opinion, is it sanitary.

Anyhow back to my thoughts about Alli. I wondered how long Alli would have continued our thing had I not flat out told him I was done. I thought about it over and over, trying to wrap my mind around it. I was so messed up emotionally that I'd even led myself to believe it was me, like I wasn't good enough for his trifling ass, but no, I had to keep reminding myself of what had happened. I recounted our conversation and how he'd been misleading me about our relationship—or better yet fling—and to think he wasn't even honest about that.

To add fuel to the fire, I had discovered the person who Allie had been in a full-blown relationship with was also his fiancé. To me, that's the highest level of misconception. I was like what? Oh, hell no, I'm not about to be involved in that type of entanglement. Another one of my mother's phrases was, "I never said a mumbling word" to him about it. I simply stopped calling him and didn't take any of his calls. He could be such an asshole. It was those types of so-called relationships that had crossed my mind from time to time, which was why I had thrown in the towel with ever knowingly partaking in another one of those meaningless casual flings again. The more I thought about it though, that sort of thing had been a pattern with me.

For one, in relationships, how was I to know what it was without getting solid clarification from the other person unless I asked? I didn't flat out ask. I acted like I was a mind reader, playing that game. I guess I figured if I knew the truth, then I couldn't unknow it. Or if I'd been straightforward, then he'd leave. Well, either way, ultimately the result was the same. The only difference was the time it took to reach that point. We could have saved each other some valuable time by saying upfront what we wanted out of our relationship.

Enough was enough, and triple enough for me, which brought me to my thoughts about Fav. I was done waiting on him, no matter what he had said—he loved me, really? Hell, I loved him far longer than he ever knew, so now because it's good for his timing, it's supposed to be good with mine too? Not this go-round. In my mind, I felt empowered and courageous, so I really thought I was done.

Time revealed a lot. It seemed pointless for me to believe there was anything other than what it was with me and Fav. Time after time, he showed me who he was and what he wanted: nothing. He didn't want anything with me. I thought if I held on and if I was patient enough, his feelings would lead him to want me more. I was fooling myself. I literally ignored all the red flags, and I knew better. He called, but not often. He sporadically texted, and in all the years, we hadn't had not one public date. Yet, I thought there was chemistry when we were together. There was no chemistry. I mistook his being good at what he did for chemistry, when in fact I'd come to realize the so-called chemistry I felt had been due to his experience. I was convinced he'd had much practice with other women. That's why he was so good.

I was amazed at how some men were able to turn on and off sexually. Most women weren't made like that—at least I wasn't. When I connected with a man regularly on a sexual basis, it became hard for me not to become emotionally attached to him. So, I knew I was addicted to Fav, but I guess the joke was on me. I was really trying to convince myself. I thought of every negative thing I could, every bad experience I'd ever had with my worst relationship. It just didn't make sense to deal with him anymore, so I made a promise to me to not go back to that. South Africa woke me up. After talking with some of the women in that culture, I learned how some of the men were accustomed to having more than one woman. Well, I live in America, and I'm not down with being part of any man's harem.

Then there was the guy I dated who, in my opinion, was a categorical womanizer. I mean, ninety percent of his friends were female. And to top that off, most of them were ex-girlfriends or so-called coworkers. Not to mention if they had children, he'd claim their offspring as his "God" children, so go figure. We got reacquainted prior to my relocation to Texas and often chitchatted on the phone. Ironically, we'd became reacquainted, and over time, we established a platonic relationship as good friends.

Funny, I never saw that relationship coming. I guess it was one of those full-circle moments where our paths crossed at the right time in our lives, and we happened to be at different phases of life. We had even reached a point where we joked about our time in the past dating each other and had even grown close enough to each other to ask our opinions about establishing relationships with other people. We seemed to have a lot in common in terms of family values, work ethic, and boundaries, and we had a good relationship that was built on respect, trust, and closeness, but that was as far as it went for me.

He was like family in a sense. Zach, India, and Shea had been introduced to him and wondered about our relationship and whether there was anything more to it, but of course I always assured them that it wasn't. I think their concern was mainly because they were afraid of me growing old alone. My children never mentioned it out loud, but I knew from some of their comments that they were trying to fix me up with someone. Even India asked me one day why I didn't consider taking him back. But then she left me alone when I finally said to her, "Well, if you are so concerned with him, then you marry him because he's no longer my type," whatever the hell that meant.

I hadn't been in a relationship in so long that I wasn't sure what my type was anymore, but I knew it wasn't him. I heard firsthand what his beliefs and what he envisioned from a relationship, and believe it or not, we were no longer on the same page. So, for me, friends it was, and friends it would ever be.

Besides, most times I'd be listening to his shenanigans about all his dates and things like that because basically a lot of the time, he would ramble on and on about himself or some other idle chatter that I rarely even knew what or who he was talking about. Bottom line, I barely got a word in edgewise. Typically, near the end of his rambling, he might ask me, "So how are you today" or "What's going on with you?" I responded with a halfhearted reply as I sensed he'd all of a sudden realized he'd been rambling.

I didn't mind though. Some of his stories were humorous, and oftentimes, I had free time to listen, so I did as a pastime. Mostly I found him quite amusing, so I looked at it as some sort of entertainment for me. He had a story for almost everything and didn't mind sharing. I'll admit, it did amaze me how much one person thought so highly of himself. *Poor thing,* I thought as I often drifted off at times as I listened to him babble on about years' past experiences when he oversaw this department or ran that business or when "they" worked for me. He often lived in the past, back in his heyday.

In my mind, I'd be thinking, *Yeah. You were fine then, but baabae, you're not all that now.* Of course, I never said as much. I would merely chuckle to myself and let him go on. I guess that's why I refer to our relationship as a full-circle moment.

In the back of my mind, I knew there had been a time when I would have driven through a snowstorm to be with him. But now, I'll just say, time had changed all that. Fast forward to the present. He was damn near handicapped and lived in an assisted living facility. I would surmise to say fate had caught up with him. He was nearly killed in a car accident several years prior. Apparently, he and his family were somewhat estranged, and the one person who was his primary caregiver was one of the many female acquaintances who lived in his nearby community. So, I guess in some respects, I felt empathy for him. Then, at other times, I literally wanted to slap his ass to the present and tell him, "Look, you might have been all that back then, but you are not it now." But hey, he was my friend, right, so I let him be great.

It was true what the elders used to say: Life is filled with swift transitions. In the blink of an eye, things can change. My friend Harmony always said I had a knack for being too nice to people, especially my exes, and I did. Even when they got on my last nerves, I would still be nice and chitchat with them.

"Whatcha doin', girl? Are you almost ready?" I'd been so lost in my thoughts, when I heard India's voice, I looked over my shoulder to see India and Shea coming through my bedroom door.

Shea was carrying two flutes of Prosecco behind India who was leading the way and carrying the bottle along with another glass. "I thought we'd have a toast to get the night started, just us girls. Here. This one is for you," India said, handing me one of the glasses.

"Why thank you. I don't mind if I do. I need to get out of this trance that I was in. I've had waaaayy too many random thoughts going on in my head. I need to relax a bit," I said as I was about to take a sip from my glass.

"Dang. I thought we were toasting. *Ummm,* Mom, we haven't even said our toast yet. You're killing our vibe, lady." Shea said as she sat on my bed with her drink.

"Oh, excuse me. Y'all go ahead then. Y'all make a toast," I said.

"Okay, I'll start..." India said as she raised her glass.

Shea cut her eyes at the both of us nonchalantly before saying, "And you'll finish 'cause y'all know I ain't 'bout that Grammy Award–winning speech makin' crap. Mom, you already know how I feel about cha, so g'on 'head, India, so we can get this party started."

I looked at Shea who already looked like she was two-thirds under the wind and shook my head while holding my glass up, anticipating India's remarks to propose her toast because I knew in my head that India wasn't going to let anything or anyone stand in the way of her dramatics. What I know for sure was we're both Pisceans and are very sensitive, and once we get on a roll, we're gone.

"Mom, I've always wanted to be at least half the woman you are today. At least at fifty percent I'd be almost as perfect as you are. Since I can remember, you have been my role model. You've never let anything or anyone stop you from doing what you've always wanted to do. Not many can say that. I'm quite sure Granny is looking down laughing and smiling at how courageous her daughter is. Mom, I'm so proud of you. I love you so much. Cheers to you," India said, raising her glass in a salute.

Shea and I both clanked our glasses to meet India's, and I felt myself getting a little misty eyed as I took another sip.

Afterward, India and I started to get dressed. Shea, being her usual self, was already dressed and was on her second drink, standing at the floor-length mirror in the corner of my room playing with her braided hair and applying more Fenty gloss to her lips. I knew we had a long night ahead of us, and the last thing I wanted was for anyone to have to rush through the Dallas traffic and rush hour as it was already six-ish. We had planned to be at the restaurant by eight, and anywhere from where we were, it would be a minimum of thirty to forty minutes to drive, and even though we had reservations, there was no sense in us being any later than what we needed to be. Knowing my family as well as I did, they always seemed to run a little behind in schedule. It was one thing to be fashionably late and another to be inconsiderate of other folks' time. Besides, in this case, it wasn't just going to be us at the dinner. India had invited a few of my Dallas friends like Maysa, Isla, Mona, and their significant others to join us as well.

"Y'all need to hurry up." After she had finally gotten her hair up in a ponytail and lip gloss on her full lips, Shea whipped around, swinging her braided twenty-inch tail dramatically like Sheneneh Jenkins from *Martin,* and said, "It don't take all that. Y'all should have been ret' ta go by now. C'mon. Let's get this show on the road, ladies. Momma gon' be sleep in a few, and India, you know how she is, so come on, y'all."

"Girl, chill. We're almost done. It might not take all that for you, Shea, but it definitely does take all that for me and Mom! 'Cause I'm just saying, we're extra all that and a bag of chips. You know how we like to be cute, girl. And tonight's extra special. We're about to be out here in these Dallas streets celebrating our momma's sixtieth, so we gotta bring it just like our momma taught us. Don't act like you don't know," India said as she was completing her look for the night.

"Whatever, girl. You're crazy, India. It's not about you tonight, so whatever. You done spent more time primping and priming yourself than Momma has. Just cut the crap and bring your crazy-tail self on. We can wait on Momma out in the car," Shea said, slurring her words.

"No one has to wait on me out in the car," I said, walking out of my bathroom into the bedroom to join Shea and India. "Has anyone talked to Zach tonight? I just want to make sure that he and Samantha are on their way and that they aren't late. India, did you give him the name of the restaurant?"

"Of course, I did, Mom. I'm not one of your other kids. You give me an assignment, and I take care of it. So, yes, Zach has the name of the restaurant and the address. If he doesn't show up on time, that's on him, but he has all the information. He's grown. He can navigate accordingly. Your son has everything he needs to be there on time, just like the rest of us. Malcolm and Zora are driving the rental car and will follow us. Let's keep the original script. I'm driving you in your car, Mom. Shea's riding with us. We're straight. I got this," India said.

"That's fine. I just want to make sure that we're all on the same page and everyone gets there on time, I just hate to have anybody waiting on us, that's all," I said to India as I walked by the mirror, taking one final admiring glance at my finished look.

"You look good, girl. Let's go," Shea said, rolling her eyes and snapping her fingers like ready, set, go.

"You don't think I have too much cleavage showing, do you?" I said as I stood looking at my reflection in the leaner mirror in my room while adjusting my boobs.

India looked at me with are-you-kidding-me look before responding, "If you're asking me, you're not showing enough. Dang, Mom. Loosen up. How are you gonna find my new stepdaddy—or should I say our new daddy—like that? I forgot. I don't want to make it all about me," India replied sarcastically as she rolled her eyes at her sister.

"Girl, for the thousandth time, let's go," Shea said before exiting the room.

"Whew, chile. Y'all getting on my nerves. Look, I don't want to play referee tonight. It's my birthday celebration. What's that y'all say? I don't need y'all being buzzkills tonight," I said as I patted my stomach and looked at my view sideways before I headed toward the bedroom door to exit.

"Buzzkills? Oh, my Lord, lady, where did you ever hear that from? I'll see you in the car," India said.

CHAPTER 9

My birthday celebration was more than I could have ever envisioned. I waltzed into the room feeling like I was above cloud nine. I was elated to see so many familiar faces, old and new, as expected. I zoomed in on Maysa, Isla, and Mona, the ladies I had become friends and silent business partners in Dallas, who were accompanied by their spouses. Standing alongside Maysa, I noticed some unfamiliar man. And much to my surprise were my girlfriends Connie, Harmony, and Suni. I was still trying to take it all in when I see Jamal and Chad, Harmony's and Connie's husbands. All I could think was, *Wow. I must really be special for the girls to bring the husbands.*

It was no secret of all the bi-annual girlfriend trips we've taken, the guys always opted out and didn't want to accompany us. To say I was elated to see them there was hardly describable. I thought, *What a night this is going to be.*

Everyone looked sensational. I knew I was experiencing the results of India's organizational and coordination skills because she'd become just as much of a stickler for details as I am when it came to hosting parties and event planning. But I also knew something of this magnitude took teamwork. I gave credit to all my children, they had really outdone themselves to have been able to pull off such a fabulous event without my knowing all the details. I was amazed when I walked in the room. I had no idea that the girlfriends were coming to the celebration. I thought it was going to be just a small gathering with only a few of the local friends I had met in Dallas and my immediate family. The decor in the room was outstanding. There were flowers and crystal centerpieces galore, and situated as a focal point in the room was a fabulous balloon arch with even more flowers. Long-stemmed roses adorned the centerpieces on the white-linen tablecloths, and gold-rimmed China place settings exquisitely sat on each table. It was like a fairytale gala affair. I couldn't have planned a better evening myself. This was going to be one for the books. India had spearheaded a picture-perfect party. I was elated and filled with joy.

At that very moment, I felt what it meant to be on top of the world. I felt as if I was floating throughout the room as I mingled and greeted various people. I hugged and received hugs; kissed and received kisses and sentiments too many to count. As the night went on, I was seated at a head table along with my immediate family. All I could think of was how glad I was that they hadn't made me the center of attention by having me sit at some table front and center all by myself. I would've wanted to sink through the floor. Honestly, as much as I liked getting dressed up and looking pretty, I did not care too much for all that attention being drawn toward me. I knew how to smile and work a crowd, but believe me, it was all a façade. I was glad when the agenda called for "dinner is served" so I could be seated and folks' attention would be off me and focused on their plates and the delectable meal that we would soon devour.

The smooth sound of music from a local jazz saxophonist permeated the entire relaxed and sophisticated ambience in the room and was at just the right level so that folks could converse and no ears were popping from too loud music and so forth. It was perfect. As we sat and ate, I swayed in my seat while listening to some of my favorites like Kem, Eric Roberson, and Avery Sunshine played in instrumental. I enjoyed a savory meal of grilled red snapper and garlic butter, asparagus, potatoes garnished with chives, and a mixture of salad greens with arugula, butter lettuce, and sweet cherry tomatoes with the lightest balsamic dressing. I even noticed some optional blue cheese crumbles—my favorite toppings—on my table in a small bowl. All I could think was, *Wow.* India made sure they nailed it with the decor. Their attention to detail was impeccable. I was well pleased, and we hadn't even gotten to the desserts or reached the program yet.

I don't know how she pulled it off, but India, little Bria, as we jokingly called her sometimes, pulled her siblings in line and managed to create a memorable experience on my behalf, and although I tried not to cry, it was difficult. My family and close friends already knew how emotional I could be, and this was one of those times. I felt my eyes well up periodically throughout the night as I sat and thought about their thoughtfulness and consideration. No one had ever done anything as nice as this for me, and even as I sat there, I was triggered by the thought that I hadn't deserved anything as beautiful as this night, and why me?

I was used to being in control and doing nice things for myself and being very generous to others. I had grown accustomed to not asking for help. I suppose this behavior stemmed from my childhood, which had taught me to be self-sufficient. In other words, I had learned to not be a bother and to be a good girl. Act right, I was taught, so for me to be vulnerable and on the receiving end of something of this magnitude—this type of external kindness—was to say the least, a bit uneasy for me. But I managed to keep my composure together while I acted like I was comfortable, jubilant, and unbothered by all the attention toward me.

All the while, my inner self was saying to me, *I can't wait for the night to progress so guests can get their drink on, dance, and enjoy the festivities where the night can be less about me.* Like I said, everything about the night was stunning, but I would have much rather had something on an intimate scale with my immediate family and a small group of close friends. As I dabbed each corner of my mouth, the waitstaff had already begun to clear the tables and bring out desserts. I was completely satisfied and full. The desserts looked amazing, and even though I was already full, I took a couple of polite bites and asked for the remainder to be wrapped to go.

Just as I was having a discourse with the waitstaff regarding having my dessert to go, I see Suni strut to a podium at the focal point of the room. I immediately looked at the dinner menu slash program, which was elegantly done with a royal-looking portrait of me silhouetted by one of my juvenile pics. Anyhow, per what I read, Suni was the hostess of ceremonies for the evening. The children had scored again. Out of the three of my girlfriends Harmony, Connie, and Suni, she was the one who had the poise and personality to expertly set the tone while keeping an audience of any type and size energized.

So far, the night had begun and was transitioning along rather nicely. My friends and family got up and said all sorts of mushy things and referenced familiar anecdotal accounts about their relationship to me, like how long they had known me, how I hadn't been a person of a lot of words, and even going as far as comparing me to the likes of E. F. Hutton, saying when I chose to speak, they generally had listened. A lot like that was said as well as them saying how I was compassionate, a good listener, a person full of wisdom, and often the voice of reason to my family and especially my girlfriends, and though much of the night was sentimental, a lot of it was humorous as well as it was entirely an enjoyable evening. I was relieved when it was all over and more relieved to see that my family was able to have a night without any drama.

I should have known that would've been too much like right though, because out of nowhere, there was an eruption coming from the back of the room near the corridor to the men's and ladies' lounge area. From what I could make out from where I stood, there appeared to be a small commotion ensuing with a few shadowy figures.

"Nah. Leave me alone. This is my momma's night. We gon' celebrate her big ol' fashion. I ain't trippin'. Y'all niggas trippin'. Leave me the fuck alone. It's a big ol' celebration. It's all about Sabria Twon, my momma. Let's celebrate."

I recognized that voice. It was my one and only son, Zach.

And just as I suspected it was indeed him, I zeroed in on Malcolm and a few other of the male guests as they all rushed to the area of the room where Zach was being surrounded and apparently subdued. Concurrently, I attempted to shift my attention from the area in question to the room to see who all might've still been in attendance to witness the fiasco. But from what I could see, it appeared Malcolm and the other men whom I'd notice from before were trying to be discreet as they attempted to escort him out the back entrance. Zach was clearly making a scene. He was jerking away from one guy to the next and flung his arms as if to say, "Leave me alone," but Malcolm put his arms around Zach as if to say, "Everything is cool," which seemed to bring Zach back to his senses. They all disappeared out the back of the venue.

It was obvious to me that he'd had too many libations during the evening, as he typically would, and in my opinion, was making an ass out of himself—and me for that matter. But nonetheless, the menfolk involved seemed to have it all in control, and as quickly as it had started, it was over.

At that point, all I could think was how glad I was that the party was over and just about all the guests had left. I suppose it was the fear of outbursts like that that made me not particularly like public celebrations. I knew from way back in the day, I'd never know what to expect from some of my family members when they were under the influence or what could and would trigger one of them to act out in public. But what I did know was that I was not going to be a part of their drama—at least not publicly.

"C'mon, birthday girl. Let me get you home before your carriage turns into a pumpkin. I know it's way past your bedtime," India said as she walked to meet me. I could tell by her expression that she was irritated by what had just transpired, but she didn't even acknowledge any of it.

"You already know," I responded.

And just like that, the excitement was gone, and the lights were dimmed, which signified it was time to go. The celebration was over. I turned to reach for my belongings from the place I'd been sitting for the night. I thought again, I was glad that we'd made it through another family-inspired event, this time with me as the focal point, without anything more happening than what had occurred with Zach's debacle. It was sad, on one hand, for me to even have had to normalize dysfunction of any kind at a public function from any family member. But that had always seemed to be the case with my family. Somebody always wanted to be seen and heard for that matter.

I was triggered again. In my mind, I retreated to my younger self, when I witnessed similar types of behavior from an alcoholic family member who had acted out publicly, which caused so much shame and embarrassment. I thought, *When will it ever end, and why can't we just be normal?*

CHAPTER 10

Had I known how different our lives were about to become in the days ahead, I might've kissed and hugged a few more of my guests, danced a little bit more, laughed a bit louder, and insisted the party lasted a bit longer, but as with most things I do, I thought logically and acted out based on what I presumed to be the right thing to do. So, I acted ladylike accordingly, pecked only a few guests on the cheeks, chuckled politely, and ended the party at a reasonable hour so as not to prolong the evening or be any more intrusive on anyone's valuable time.

I'm not a fortune teller. There was no way for me to predict the future. I do have some discernment and can usually pick up on when things are not obviously clear. I, like most people, do what I believe to be the right thing to do without using any clairvoyance. I make the best of situations as they occur and realize there is no sense in living with a bunch of would'ves, should'ves, and could'ves. I prided myself on living in the present and embracing it, and what I knew for certain was all we have is the now, and tomorrow is not promised. That for sure was the one thing that had been rooted and grounded in my upbringing.

I understand how imperative it was to embrace every precious moment, the perfect and imperfect times. One thing my momma always said that stuck with me was, "What a difference a day makes," and I swear, the older I get, the more I realize those words were not a cliché, but they were a statement of fact.

I knew I couldn't control the things that Zach did—he was a grown man—yet as his mother, I couldn't get over the fact that I wanted to talk with him and ask him what his problem was. What had happened at my party wasn't the first time that Zach had acted out in public. The only difference was this time, I was just sick of it. I wanted to get to the bottom of it, and like India said, I knew I wasn't to blame for his behavior, but I didn't feel I had done my due diligence if I hadn't tried to have an honest conversation with him. I reached for my phone to give him a call. I looked at the time. It's nine-eleven a.m. I knew he wouldn't be awake yet, but I didn't care. Now was as good a time as any.

"Hello, Zach. It's me," I spoke into the phone.

"Good morning, Mom. How you doing?" Zach responded.

"I'm good. I'm calling to see where your head is. What was going on with you last night?" I asked, trying as best as I could not to lose my cool.

"Oh, man…nothing really…I was just trying to enjoy…*ummm*…you know…you know how I do sometimes. I have a little too much to drink, and I get a little carried away," Zach said in a froggish hungover-sounding voice.

"Yeah, I understand the...you wanting to enjoy yourself part. For that matter, we all wanted to enjoy ourselves. The part I'm referring to is the getting carried away. At some point, it gets to be a little too much, even for you. You need to start taking into consideration the feelings of others and the impact your belligerent behavior has. Not to mention the fact that you might even consider taking better care of yourself. How about you think about what you're doing and how it affects your relationships? Let me put it bluntly: your relationship with me.

"Last night wasn't supposed to be about you, honey. It was about you supporting and celebrating me and my birthday, and I'm just gonna be honest with you: My feelings were a bit hurt in that you couldn't restrain yourself and conduct yourself appropriately. Listen, you drink as much as you want. I can't tell you what to do about that, but I can control my space, and what I need is this: In the future, I'm asking you not to come around if you believe you can't manage your alcohol intake. I need you to respect my request. I love you and want to be around you, but not when you're drunk, that's nonnegotiable for me," I said.

"Mom, really, no disrespect, but damn. You know, I don't know what you expect from me. It is so hard trying to please you. Your bar is so high. All I was trying to do was have a good time. I wasn't trying to embarrass you. Don't nobody promote or salute you like I do, so I'm hurt for you to think that I work Monday through Friday and sometimes Saturday, and just because I choose to kick it like I do, that it's a direct shot at you to bring you down. I don't ask you for anything, but anything you need, I got you, but I feel like it's never enough for you. How are you always so hard on me? It's like I'm this great big disappointment to you. Am I, Mom? Am I a disappointment to you? Everything I do seems to embarrass you. You're never happy with anything I do, but let it be India or Shea. They can do anything, and nothing's ever said. So, what if I have one too many drinks. You look at me as if I'm an outcast. I'm done. I dunno, I'm just done. But I get it. You won't have to worry 'bout me embarrassing you anymore, bet. I gotta go. Talk to you later," Zach said, and before I could reply to him, the call had disconnected.

I felt the anguish in his voice, and it hit like a ton of bricks right straight to my heart. I had not expected that out of him. At that moment, I chose not to call my son back. Sometimes it's better to give things time and not address them right away so they don't become any worst. And I was feeling like this was definitely a case scenario I needed to soak on. From the sounds of it, this wasn't solely about the drinking, and what happened at my party sounded like there was a deeper issue going on. I knew in my mind, I wasn't going to ignore this.

The last thing I wanted to do was to alienate my children from me. I might not agree with everything they did or how they lived their lives, but I loved them and knew we'd figure out how to have a relationship with each other. We always seemed to figure out how to overcome our differences—we always had. I believed this thing with Zach and me was going to take some time. Zach was no longer a child, that was one thing I knew for sure. It wasn't like I could spank him and send him to his room. No, he was an adult who needed some emotional support on a deeper level. Whatever his issues were, I hoped he would be able to get the help he needed. Therapy had helped me heal from a lot of my own childhood trauma, so somehow, I was hoping Zach would do the same. At the same time, I needed to understand that I couldn't make him get the help he needed, nor did I want to demean him for not living up to my expectations. Yeah, I thought, this is going to take some time for us to work through.

For many years, I battled feelings of failure, embarrassment, anger, and shame. I had naively believed that good parenting resulted in good kids. Foolishly, I had convinced myself that had all my children had the same father, been reared in a two-parent household, they'd have turned out to be damn-near perfect. So, when my children acted out, it felt like a reflection on me as a mom. I had to learn to let go of that assumption. I had to let go of the stigma against being a single African American mother. I had to let go of my idea of who my children should be and embrace who my children were.

As time went on, I grew stronger with the aid of many self-help books, therapy, and most of all my faith and belief in God. I had learned to let go and not be so unforgiving on myself. I never let go of setting goals and reaching them, but I let go of my unrelenting quest of expectations from my children that the outcomes of their lives was an adverse reflection of me. I had finally come to the realization that I had done everything I could to be the best mother I could be for my children, and I learned to let go of what was out of my control. I couldn't parent or love the choices Zach, India, or Shea made away. Each of them had been taught right from wrong, so how they chose to live their lives was on them. I had to accept, validate, and empathize with them if they needed me. At the same time, I had to choose to protect my own mental state by allowing them to live their lives as they deemed appropriate. At the end of the day, it included coming to the heartbreaking acceptance that some things in this life were simply out of my control.

CHAPTER 11

I was still trying to process the last conversation I'd had with Zach. I didn't know if he knew it or not, but I was really starting to lose my patience with him. He was too old not to be taking accountability for the messes he'd caused with relationships between those who were near and dear to him. It seemed like the more I brought it to his attention, the more likely he'd been to twist it around and portray himself as the victim.

I suppose age doesn't make a person mature. I began to realize my son didn't have the emotional maturity or mental capacity to make better decisions, otherwise he would have. Zach was a Leo, and true to form, he had a very selfish nature. But then again, that's from a Zodiac sign perspective. In reality, signs and stuff like that didn't matter to me. I don't know where that random thought even came from. I supposed I'd been thinking about a conversation I'd previously had with Maysa. She was always bringing up Zodiac signs and the compatibility of this sign to that one. Hell, if I'd lived my life by that measure, I wouldn't have had most of the relationships I'd been in.

Essentially, I had to accept the realization I was Zach's mother and had done what I could to raise him. I couldn't raise a grown man. It was up to him to make better choices in life. I wanted him to change his behavior. Those were things I wanted for him. He had to want it for himself though. All this thinking about my family had become mentally exhausting for me.

I refused to allow Zach or anyone else for that matter to inflict guilt on me. I said what I said, and that was it. If Zach didn't respect my boundaries, then oh well. I needed to do what I had to do to protect my own mental space. I'm not saying I had been perfect, but I had to give myself some grace. Lord knows I'd been through enough childhood trauma of my own to know not to play victim and to know when someone was trying to manipulate me with mind games.

My thoughts were interrupted by a knock on the bedroom door. I glanced at my phone, and it displayed nine twenty-one. I had laid in bed longer than usual.

"Mom, are you awake?" India asked.

"Yes, I am. Come on in," I responded. India walked in and climbed on the bed, sitting cross-legged at the foot.

"So, Shea and I were going over the events from last night, and we think Zach needs a family intervention."

"Well, don't look at me. I'm not being a part of no damn intervention. I've had it with that type of thing. Don't y'all remember the last intervention we all did? As a matter of fact, if memory serves me right, it was with Shea. Now ain't that the pot calling the kettle black? How easily we forget when the shoe is on the other foot," I said, looking at India side eyed.

"Yeah, I guess that didn't go over so well that last time. But look how it all turned out in the long run. Shea got her life back on track, and even though it might not have seemed like it then, she eventually turned her life around. I think our intervention did have something to do with it to some degree. Mom, listen, you might not realize it, but we do pay attention to what you have to say. We hear you. I know it doesn't seem like we do, but we do. I mean for real, for real, we hear you. Not everyone has a mom like you. I mean, some of my friends don't even have elders in their family that they can get good, sound advice from," India said.

"Yeah, well, it's a wonder I have any more good sound advice to give. I feel like I'm poured out and have nothing left in me. For one thing, y'all send me off as the bad guy and make it look like I'm the one prying in so-called grown-up business, and I'm tired of it. Zach has been taught better; he's doing what he wants to do. Anyhow, I've already had a conversation with him about respecting other folks' boundaries, and that's all I care to discuss with him for now. I suggest you and Shea do the same. We don't need a family intervention to do that. Everyone just needs to speak up for themselves and take accountability for how they want to be treated. I love all of you, and I told you time and time again how much I disapprove of talking about one child behind the other one's back. I don't want to be a part of that. Whatever you and

Shea have going on with Zach, you need to address it with him. Otherwise, he'll think we're all just ganging up on him, especially Shea. She goes along with Zach's bullshit, then behind his back, she'll talk about how embarrassed she was by something he's said or done. No, it's time out for that. And where is Shea? I need her to be a part of this conversation as well," I said, adjusting the pillows between me and the headboard. I needed to support my back and sit upright for how I was about to be sent off a cliff by Shea and India.

Nevertheless, I felt the weight of the world on my shoulders. All I ever wanted was for them all to love one another unconditionally. I wanted them to have a bond better than any relationship I'd ever had with any of my siblings. No sooner than those feelings of guilt started to creep in, I shuddered at the thought of what I wanted and forced myself to come back to reality. I consciously knew I'd been triggered by this whole conversation with India. And it was at that moment when I began to think, *It is what it is, so don't go making this more than that.*

My daughters thought I didn't know what they were up to, but I did. It wasn't only my girls though; all my children had a knack for deflecting situations as it pertained to them specifically. This time it was Shea and India teaming up against Zach. Most times it was Team Zach and Shea against India.

"Shea FaceTimed me this morning. She didn't stay here last night. She and Zora got a room because they went to some rooftop party in Deep Elum. But yeah, pass your phone. I'll get her on

FaceTime again. You're right. She needs to hear this too," India said as I tossed her my phone.

"Right. So, she can hear this shit right from the horse's mouth. I ain't doing no damn intervention. That's a negative," I said.

My house was noiseless and felt so peaceful. I was alone listening to my own sounds and the occasional notifications from my phone, laptop, and the furnace. For some reason, I hadn't even asked Alexa to play Anita Baker, XM radio, or anything. I was basking in the moment and embracing the peace and quiet. I wasn't doing anything in particular, just sort of piddling around the house, straightening up around my living room, looking around with a sense of gratitude at my surroundings while trying to decide on what I should have for lunch. Randomly, I recapped the last couple of days when my family had been present—things like how we interacted with one another crossed my mind. I laughed silently thinking about Suni, Harmony, and Connie and how they each had teased me about showing all my cleavage at my birthday dinner party. I reminisced on how good it had been to see everyone.

The kids had all said their good-byes and were all on their way back to each one's respective destination. It was always a good time having my children with me again. I had enjoyed them, but again, as always, it was a warm feeling loving on them in person, and it was okay to see them go. We had our ups and downs, and just like any other thing we'd been through, somehow or another, this thing with Zach would eventually work itself out. I was sure of it. I just didn't know how exactly things would play out or when. And no matter how firm I stood on not being to blame and Zach being responsible for his actions, in the corridors of my mind, I still couldn't seem to contain the dusty remnants of Zach's issues out of my head. Right now, I was torn between protecting my own mental state and the progress I'd made in my therapy sessions versus relapsing to my old behavior patterns, the motherly instinct that lured me into wanting to fix my son's problems and save him from his own self-destruction.

CHAPTER 12

March 2020

Saying desperate times called for desperate measures was no longer a cliché but an actual thing. All over, folks had become anxious, to say the least. I mean, I got it. Fear of the unknown can be a beast. We were shut down all across the world. Folks were running around stocking up on toilet paper, paper towels, and disinfectant spray and wipes. All of us were wearing masks just to go to the grocery store.

Hell, for that matter, some of us were afraid to go to the grocery store.

The first few weeks of the coronavirus shutdown, Shea sent a pic of the roads in Rockford, Illinois. It literally looked like a ghost town. And it was at two in the afternoon. Talk about strange. I never would have imagined in my lifetime that I would have lived in a time called a pandemic.

It was after we'd celebrated my birthday that all hell seemed to break loose. Isla's client Miss Emma's doctor had been right. The coronavirus had hit the United States in January of 2020, but no one in my direct circle seemed to believe it was as serious as it was. Otherwise, I doubt we would've had a gathering in February.

It was around mid-March when the news media started informing the public about the outbreak. In Dallas, most of our large malls, like the Galleria, North Park, and stores like Nordstrom's and Macy's started shutting down. Churches across the nation closed their doors, and small businesses closed.

Diva's shutdown completely. Maysa, Isla, and Mona didn't know what was going to happen to their businesses. The one saving grace for the church I attended was when the pastor started a daily morning virtual six o'clock prayer call. I don't know how I would have made it without that connection to my faith and other people. It wasn't as if I had anyone to spend time with during the pandemic because I lived alone.

Life changed for everyone I knew. In the midst of the pandemic, communication among my three closest girlfriends, Harmony, Connie, and Suni dwindled to a rare occurrence, as the chaotic waves of uncertainty seemed to distance us even in the digital realm. I would have thought that because most folks were using digital platforms, such as social media, messaging apps, or video call, that our relationship would have continued to flourish during the dismal times of the pandemic. But such didn't seem to be the case with us. Instead, we'd all begun to experience more of a differing of opinion for all the wrong reasons. Stuff that I used to let roll off my back had started to unnerve me and them. We were all on edge. I'd never been the one to verbally express my opinion about religion and politics, but things seemed to have gone awry during the pandemic.

Every channel on television featured some allegedly expert panel discussion about a conspiracy theory related to the virus, as it was called. Social media posts were extreme and disrespectful. Folks I had considered friends were coming across with extremists viewpoints. It was insane, and there was an overwhelming deluge of political misinformation during that time, clouding public discourse with confusing and baseless narratives. Spearheading a lot of the rhetoric came directly from the current president and his racist antics. I literally had to unfollow some friends on social media because of their posts and our difference of opinion about the president, his thoughts, and the fallout of the virus.

Amid the pandemic, the president's divisive remarks fueled a surge in violence and hate crimes, with public perception swayed by conflicting news sources. The confusion extended to the legitimacy of the COVID virus itself, despite scientists consistently providing the American people with crucial information about COVID-19 transmission preventative measures like mask wearing and social distancing, vaccine development, and emerging variants. Scientists also emphasized the importance of hand hygiene and shared insights on the virus impact on different age groups and pre-existing conditions, there was continuous research updates and public health guidelines all of which were key in managing the pandemic. In contrast, conspiracy theories cast doubt on the virus's origin, preventative measures, and the efficacy of COVID vaccines, causing vast confusion and chaos amongst the public.

Tragically many people lost their lives due to the COVID-19 virus during the pandemic. The global impact was substantial with millions of reported deaths attributed to the virus, the severity varied, and efforts to mitigate the spread and develop vaccines were critical in addressing the crisis. And as if that wasn't enough to deal with, hearing the news of the prevalence of killings of black men and women around the country, and the real cause of the pandemic had gotten way out of hand. It was no wonder people had gotten so desperate acting in behavior. Personally, I think a lot of it had to do with the ambiguity of the virus. We didn't know how long we'd be shut down. First, it started out as a two-week period, then a month, then two months, some cases longer. People seemed to literally be going crazy in anguish and despair.

"Girl, if I get another message from someone sending me a text about starting an online business or sending me a link to a Zoom meeting about how to get a new form of income or about how to get multiple streams of income, or how to build generational wealth, I'm going to lose it," I said to Maysa as we were chatting on the phone one week during the shutdown. I had reached out to Maysa to see how things were going since her business had been closed down.

"Yeah, I know what you mean. But real talk, I got in one of those schemes. Girl, you'll be surprised at how many people are on those calls. Hell, a girl gotta do what a girl gotta do. I at least wanted to know if it worked," Maysa said.

"Girl, I don't trust anything. I have to pay money to make money, especially not with a group of Black folks—not a group of White ones either. I learned my lesson years ago about get-rich-quick opportunities. They generally don't work, so I'll stick to what I know," I said.

I was referring to a time back in the day when I went to work for a guy who claimed I and whoever joined his pyramid insurance investment business could work our way to become wealthy—because the head of the team, Joe Blow, who was at the top of the pyramid was wealthy, so why wouldn't it work for anyone else? Well, guess what? It didn't, and I had to pay a hefty tax bill and lost thousands of dollars as a result of it. So, no thanks to any get-rich-quick deals for me. I didn't want to be the Debbie Downer for Maysa, so I let her go on about the pyramid scheme she had gotten herself involved in. I figured she'd eventually find out for herself the real benefit of it.

"They're not pyramid schemes. They're called boards. Girl, I heard my friends, the Travises just bought a house, and all their family members are on the calls. I believe they have been making money, so I'm going to hang in there and see where it takes me," Maysa said, she was insistent and was trying her best to convince me to join.

"Nah, girl. I'll pass. I've had so many people reach out to me that it's gotten to the point where I was leery of opening text messages or phone calls for that matter from folks I hadn't heard from in a while because I no longer wanted to be propositioned for any more frivolous offers. So, if you and I are going to remain friends, please don't ask me again, because I am not interested. Zach even reached out to me, trying to get me to join one of those groups back home. I had to school my kids on that shit too. But I knew they'd know better, because anything risking them losing their money, is a hard no.

My girl Connie and I are barely on speaking terms now because she's so deep into the shit. I find it all ridiculous, but she believes it's going to build her family's generational wealth. I said okay, let me know how it works out for you. I just think people are desperate and will do anything in times like these," I said to Maysa, and I meant every word. As for me and my money, I'll stick with a financial planner. I'm not Cash App-ing shit to no damn body.

CHAPTER 13

January 2021

"Miss Bria, I am so outdone. I learned terms I didn't realize existed prior to 2020. Hell, I learned my love interest, the man I thought was of the man of my dreams was quarantining with his ex. What the hell? I mean did he actually think it was okay with me? I was so damn tired of hearing the phrase *You teach people how to treat you* during COVID-19. He was sending me dick pics via text message. I was sending pics of my private parts. I thought we had a thing going. Damn! Here I go again, ignoring the signs. Was it coincidental that most of the phone calls I received from him were while he was in his car on the way to pick up food from restaurants."

"What? Are you kidding me? I'm over it already!!" Maysa was nearly screaming into the phone.

"Yeah. One thing is for sure: This pandemic has uncovered quite a few of folks' hidden agendas. I've seen enough racism, systematic injustice, inequality for all, and cheating men on a whole new level to last me a lifetime. I just thought I'd throw that last part in to get a chuckle out of you, girl. But seriously, I'm sorry to hear your boo was under quarantine with his ex. Did you ask what the reason for that was? Maybe it was to make it convenient for the kids' caregiving needs or something of that nature. You said they have joint custody of their children, so maybe there's more to it than what you know. I think you should allow him to explain because you both seem to have a decent relationship before the pandemic," I said, trying to offer my friend the best sounding voice of reason that I could.

I knew how desperate Maysa seemed to be in wanting things to work out between her and this new guy she had been seeing. I was happy she'd found someone who seemed to be treating her the way she deserved to be treated in a relationship. And I also had gotten to know my friend well enough to know that sometimes she could be a little bit over the top, especially as it related to relationships.

Maysa had had a few bad relationships in the past and found it difficult to trust anyone. Knowing her like I do, there was a slight chance she was overreacting. I didn't know, but until I heard her out, I couldn't rush to judgment. And, on the other hand, I didn't want to probe her too much either. As a supportive friend, I realized sometimes all a person wanted and needed was a safe place to vent their frustration and for someone to just listen. So, unless she asked for my opinion, I wasn't giving it.

"He didn't actually say that they were together, but that's how it sounded. I don't know. I didn't want to ask too many questions 'cause things have been going so good, and I don't want to come off as being too clingy and shit. It's only been a little over a year since we've been dating. In fact, our first date was at your party back in February, and here it is January 2021. I'm an emotional wreck. Can you believe our president incited his supporters to an insurrection against our nation, which led to other extremists' riots, and elected officials, Cicely Tyson died and Hank Aaron... It's too much already." Maysa sounded like she was about to burst into tears.

"Damn, you *are* a wreck. You might be overreacting. I'm just saying—and not to change the topic...*ummm*—I didn't realize the deaths of Miss Tyson and Mr. Aaron bothered you that much. I know as of late, things are happening so suddenly and making us all feel some type of way about it. But damn, pull it together, girl. We still have to remember this is the progression of life. We just have to put life in perspective, but on a lighter note, if I were to put my life in perspective at this moment, I'd have to calculate how many bottles of Pinot I had drank during this damn pandemic. There was a saying, *Every little bit adds up.* I know a little equals a lot over time. Now this could be a good and a bad thing depending on someone else's perspective. If I was setting goals, doing a little each day toward reaching a positive goal would be a relatively good thing. Now as I put it into perspective, to where I am as it related to drinking more during this traumatic time, drinking an ounce of Pinot on the hour by the hour was not

121

so much a good thing. I have concluded that I needed to be mindful of all the drinking I've done over time. And I realized it had become obsessive. I may sound like I'm rambling but the essence is that the emotional strain we're experiencing can push us toward excesses we'd otherwise approach with moderation. With that summation in mind, I decided to make an appointment to start my mental therapy again. It might not be a bad idea for you to consider doing the same," I said.

"Where in the hell did you come up with that shit? I must be just as crazy as you, 'cause I actually understood what you said and yeah, you might be right. This damn pandemic has changed our normal so much. Hell, people have even started to talk differently. More often, I'm hearing terms like *navigating, pivoting, channeling,* and the one phrase I'm so sick of hearing is the *new normal.* Excuse me for saying this, but *fuck* the new normal. I mean what the hell was wrong with the old normal? Can we just have that mug back? I'm sick of this shit," Maysa said, and we both burst into laughter.

I don't know if we were laughing to keep from crying. But what Maysa said was dead on. Everyone seemed to need some type of mental therapy. The pandemic had really taken a toll on folks. One thing I will say though, being confined to my home during long periods of time certainly gave me the chance to become more self-aware. I knew once I started my biweekly virtual therapy sessions I'd feel even better. I feel like I have gotten to know myself in ways I hadn't ever in my past. I found I had a low tolerance for nonsense. I learned what made me tick—I mean really tick. I learned to accept myself for me and not be afraid of what others thought. I think that was the silver lining in the pandemic for my relationships as well. I'd shared my similar thoughts with India during one of our weekly chats.

"We were forced in a sense to spend time with ourselves for once in our lives without any distractions. Some days I would just sit in silence. No phone calls to anyone. It was like what more was there to discuss? I was sick of talking about the current president and politics. Hell, for that matter, I didn't know like most people. We didn't know who was going to die from COVID-19 next. We witnessed so many deaths from the disease, so the last thing on my mind was to sit and discuss negativity," I said to India during our FaceTime chat.

"I know what you mean, Mom. I had decided if I was on my last days then I wanted to make the best of it and live my best life. So, with that in mind, I started to wean myself from what I believed to be toxic vibes and energy in my life. Malcolm hates all the stones and smells I have going in the house now. Things and people that were draining had to go—no more. That meant family, too, if they were draining. I decided to love them from a distance—that was until I received a phone call that my bestie Julie had contracted the virus," India said.

"Yeah. That must have made it real for you. I remember how hesitant I'd become to answer the phone at certain times of the night. I was afraid someone from our family was calling to say someone had contracted the virus, or it was someone calling to say another person had died from it," I said.

"I know, right? I hadn't talked to Julie in a while, and when I saw her name pop up, I immediately got nervous. She and I had not spoken in a few months because she has a new boo, and you know how my friend does, when she gets a new boo, she becomes distant from her friends. Not only that, but for whatever reason, we just didn't see eye to eye on things and had different perspectives on life in general, so it seemed best for us to love one another from a distance," India said.

"Yeah, I get it. There seems to be a lot of that going on within relationships—family and friends both. I think it was mainly due to everyone being on edge. All of us could benefit from some mental support. I, for one, am a strong advocate of it. This is and was new to all of us. I mean that's why you went and got the emotional support pet, right?" I said to India.

"Yeah, and when I first told Malcolm that was what I needed, he thought I was dang near losing my mind for sure, but it was either that or I was going to start smoking weed, using edibles, or drinking. I didn't want to do any of those things, so the dog was the next best option," India said, chuckling.

"My crazy-ass friend Suni has been using edibles. She says they help her sleep. Suni will try anything though, and she thinks I don't know, but I know she and Trace, her neighbor, still smoke weed from time to time. I just shake my head at her. She was smoking weed before the pandemic, so I know her old ass is smoking it now. But yeah, I get what you're saying. Do what you have to do, but please do so within reason. We've had enough alcoholics in our family, so I don't need you added to the list. I'm still trying to get Zach's ass to get help for the error of his ways. The last I heard from Shea, he's been up to his usual crap," I said.

"Don't even tell me about it, Mom. I can't with him right now," India said.

CHAPTER 14

A few days had gone by, and I hadn't talked to Maysa. The shutdown had everybody tripping. First thing I was going to get back to was walking. The sun was shining bright when I looked out my window, so I decided I'd put on my workout attire. I grabbed a sports bra, a loose t shirt, some leggings, a pair of footies, and my sneakers. After I'd put on my gear, went to the bathroom, washed my face and stuff, and brushed my teeth, I knew a good four-mile walk along the bike trail in my condo complex was just what I needed to clear my head. As I was about to exit my door, my phone rang. I looked at it, and I saw it was Maysa. I answered without hesitation.

"Hey, girl. How are you doing?" I answered.

"Hey, girl. I'm good. Whatchu up to?" Maysa asked.

"Girl, I'm about to head out for a walk. So, are you feeling better since the last time we talked? You sound better. I take it things worked out for the good between you and your boo about his quarantining with his ex," I said.

"Yeah, girl. It's much better. Girl, I had to call you to tell you I overreacted alright. It turns out, I was wrong. He wasn't with her and the kids. I so misunderstood. I'm so ashamed of myself for that. Anyhow, we talked, and all is good. You don't want to know what I'm up to now though," Maysa said with more enthusiasm in her voice as she snickered. By the sounds of her voice, I sensed she was up to no good.

"Well, tell me, girl. How's the relationship going with your boo? And I want all the details, girl. This shutdown got us all living vicariously through one another the best way we can. Go on ahead and spill it, girl," I said.

"He is so sweet to me. It seems so unreal. I asked him how he felt about coming to meet me at the store so I could pick up some items for the house, you know just to get out for a bit. His response was, 'I got you.' I said what do you mean, and he said, 'I've got you. Whatever it is you need, I got you.' He said those other niggas stupid. I ain't going nowhere.' He said an ex is an ex for a reason. I don't roll like that. If I say I got you, I mean it. I don't say what I don't mean. Oh my God, Ms. Bria, I think I'm in love with this dude. I just can't believe how much we vibe," Maysa said.

"Well, I gotta say, I'm exceedingly happy for you. And you better believe it 'cause you certainly deserve it—every piece of it. See, sometimes we subject ourselves to dysfunctional relationships for so long that we begin to believe it's normal, then when something different comes along, we don't know how to accept it. We resist and struggle with being in a mutually loving compatible, and drama-free relationship because we've grown so accustomed to being in drama," I said.

"I also want to say thank you for listening and allowing me to share my joy with you. Anybody else would have felt like I was overreacting and wondering why I go on so much about him, so I appreciate you listening to me. I'm just so freakin' happy, I can't believe it," Maysa said.

"Girl, I don't mind living vicariously through your happiness. You're a reminder to me that's what love looks like and should be like. What I know is this: We women are not afraid of showing love when it's reciprocated. We just don't want to be made fools out of, so when the right guy comes along and he's not afraid to show love, honey, we're all in. So, yes, thank you for sharing your love story with me. Who doesn't want love? We all do. I'm ecstatic for you. So, what else are you up to? You must be on some foolery over there," I said jokingly.

"Girl, you know I am. I'm over here making porn videos and trying to edit my fat-ass stomach out of 'em so I can send a pic to my boo," she said, laughing out loud at her own foolishness.

"*Ooooh,* TMI. Girl, shut up. Well, I'mma tell you what, that man ain't gon' care nothing about that stomach in them videos, I can promise you that," I said.

"Miss Bria, girl, you are one crazy chick." Maysa laughed back at me.

"Oh, I'm crazy, but you're ova there editing porn videos. Yeah, okay. That's alright, girl. You gotta do whatchu gotta do. I ain't mad at you. Hell, I wish I had somebody to send a pic, video, or something to. I'd be doing the exact same thang. It's rough out here in these single streets," I replied.

"You got that right, honey, 'cause this whole damn pandemic thing got us all in a whole different mind space. Who would have known at dang near fifty years old my ass would be sending my private parts electronically? Funny, huh?" Maysa said.

"Yeah, but even funnier than that, but real talk, who would've known we would've been in a damn shutdown for almost two damn years, you know what I mean?" I said in a more serious tone.

"Yeah, girl, you're absolutely right. You know it's all I can do these days to keep my mental state together," Maysa said.

"You're damn straight. That seems to be the going topic these days. That's why I'm not judging anybody for anything they gotta do to keep it together, as long as it's legal. You feel me?" I spoke.

"What's up with you, girl? You good? Have you heard anything from Fav?" Maysa asked.

"I'm good, and to your question, yes. We've been in touch with each other, believe it or not. I finally gave in and called him to say, 'just checking on you and miss you.' That was all it took, and like clockwork, we've been going strong ever since. So yeah, I'm good," I said.

"Okayyy…that's so wonderful. It's about time your stubborn tail turned around," Maysa said.

"Yeah, well, we can give credit to this damn pandemic mess. It's got all of us thinking about life from another angle. I know him. I'm not so sure I feel like teaching someone new how to be with me. I don't want to sound like I'm settling either. Fav and I have had our challenges, that's for sure. For the most part, we get one another. I've changed and so has he," I said.

There had been so much more to my and Fav's conversations as we grew closer during the pandemic. I hadn't realized I was the one shutting him out. He let me know that there were times he'd try to show me how he felt, and I seemed to intentionally sabotage our relationship. I thought about it and discussed it with my therapist, and one of the things that I learned about my behavior was that my reactions stemmed from being raised by an emotionally immature parent. I was surprised to learn how much childhood trauma experiences carried over into adult relationships. I had experienced so much childhood trauma, which impacted my relationships with others that I hadn't realized it. It wasn't only my intimate relationships; it was all people relationships. I learned in therapy that I had learned to cope by developing what in therapy is called an internalizer.

The more I went through my own healing process, I began to realize how emotionally immature I was with my own children. Yes, I had made so many mistakes with them. It wasn't too late for me to take ownership for my role in my past mistakes with them and most importantly for me to acknowledge it verbally to each of them. One of the biggest takeaways I got out of my therapy was that it was healthy and okay to admit where I felt like I dropped the ball. Doing nothing kept me in the same place. I needed to be honest with myself and them to help our relationships grow. In therapy, it took many sessions before I unpeeled the onion to get to my real self versus my imaginary role self.

The therapy journey was a process, and it would take much time for me to learn about myself to help me evolve and reach a point of healing. I was still a work in progress, and I was ready and willing to do whatever it took to continue my process toward being a better me. My life depended on it, and I mattered.

CHAPTER 15

There was something calming about a morning walk and the sounds of birds chirping in the atmosphere. I was surrounded by the clouds in the distant sky; the sun shone bright. There wasn't anything I appreciated more other than being at an ocean front. Nothing calmed me more than walking first thing in the morning. I got lost in my thoughts, and as usual, it gave my mind clarity and gave me a sense of peace. I loved seeing the beautiful red tulips, yellow daffodils, and the lavender flowers along my path and the early blooms on the trees. Since the pandemic had begun, I realized I was not okay mentally. Since I had not seen Fav in person in quite some time, I had to admit I was getting a little horny being away from him.

We talked regularly via phone, video chat, and text, so that was an improvement. On the home front, things had been a bit challenging. I could no longer go to the gym because everyone was quarantining, and the thought of wearing a mask during a workout made me claustrophobic. Thank God for electronics and virtual conferencing and FaceTime devices. Even with all of that, life got a bit daunting at times. Using creativity, we all learned how to reach out and touch virtually. We had to. Otherwise, I know we would have been entirely disconnected from one another.

No one came right out and spoke about how they felt. I knew they were just as bothered as I was. Zach, of course, had been drinking more. India and Malcolm were pretty much quarantined together. Shea was quarantined in her own space, and Zora was with some friends.

I just prayed no one got COVID-19 and we all remained healthy. I knew it was hard for the young folk. They didn't like being told to stay home or to wear masks. All of it was a real trip, but that's how it was, so that was that. I felt a sense of peace. I had learned to manage my present by taking daily walks and exercising at home. It was surprising to me how much clearer my mind was and how much better I felt, not only mentally, but physically and overall. The small things that used to affect me no longer did.

I had also been giving more thought about how I was going to approach my children. I knew it had to be done for healing to begin. In fact, after discussing it with my therapist, she recommended it would be a good accountability homework assignment to help me recognize my weaknesses in that area and for me to reinforce different communication techniques used with my children. Funny, this didn't just come up. I've always felt there was an elephant in the room where Zach and my relationship was concerned. I just didn't know the right approach to take to address it. Now I know I just didn't have the capacity to handle emotional rearing with my children. I thought I was doing the right thing by supporting their basic needs, like putting a roof over their heads and making sure they had food and clothes. I didn't think I'd neglected their emotional needs. I didn't know because I hadn't received that from my own parents. *Wow,* I thought, *once you know better, Sabria Twon, you can't unknow what you know.*

As I was walking along, I also thought about what I'd told Maysa. Yeah, Fav and I had been going pretty strong virtually ever since I'd finally drummed up the courage to return his call. I chuckled recalling the day he returned my text. I had received a notification on my Apple Watch, which I initially dismissed thinking it was the typical spam text because it came through so early. I never bothered to even check because I didn't want to break my pace. I thought, *I'll address it later,* but low and behold, when I decided to look at the screen, I saw an old, familiar area code and a message that read, *I miss you. I need to be inside you.* And just like that, there I was right back, like I never left. In my mind, I couldn't turn without him being in my every thought. Foolish or not, at that moment, not only did it resonate what I heard him say, more relevantly, it reminded me of how much I missed him, his touch, and I wanted him inside me, and just the thought of that made me wet. That thought made me smile.

Days later, Shea called to discuss an issue she was having with her girlfriend Corliss moving in. I swear sometimes my children believed I was their switchboard operator of life. Hypothetically, all my retired life consisted of was waiting on them to call me to resolve all their problems. And then, on the other hand, I guess it was good to be needed in that way. It wasn't like I solved their problems for them. It was more of me providing a safe place for them to talk whatever issue out loud without judgment—well sometimes, without judgment—but most times, I offered a good voice of reasoning, and they generally figured it out themselves. After some time, I evolved to the point of watching them figure it out though, and that's why I am a strong believer in therapy.

"Think in terms of boundaries when determining whether you want someone to live with you, Shea. Be practical. It's more to it than what you believe. What's your vision? Are you lonely, or do you need help with a bill? But think it all the way through. And whatever you decide, keep it even because at the end of the day, what does it benefit you, and what does it benefit her? If your long-term goals are not compatible to the short-term fix or equate to the payoff you get by moving in together, then you might reconsider that idea. Are you sure you're ready for that type of commitment? Hell, write it out. Remember my lists? Write in terms of positive versus the negative," I said.

Back in the day when I reared my children, I used to be keen on making them write lists. I had forgotten about it until one day India reminded me of it. She said she swears by it to this day when faced with certain aspects and decisions in her life. It works.

"See, Corliss says we should move in together because it'll be cheaper for us and since we spend so much time together anyway that we might as well live together. But to me, that's just the over for the under," Shea said.

"What do you mean, when you say that's just the over for the under?" I asked.

"Like she is basically saying something to cover up what her true intentions are. In other words, I know there's more to it than what she says is the reason she wants us to move in together. Sometimes she's too clingy. Yeah, we spend a lot of weekend outings together, but through the week, I'm about working and being focused on that. I don't have time to be all booed up under nobody like that," Shea explained.

"Oh, okay, I'm following you now. I'll try to offer help and support without always being the problem solver. The best recommendation I'll make is I'll ask you to consider what your needs are before you make your final decision," I said to Shea while cringing at the T.M.I. she so freely shared.

"Well, I've been trying to consider my needs first. I'm tired of always giving in to someone else's needs before mine," Shea said sounding exasperated.

As I listened to Shea, I believed in my heart of hearts that she would make the best decision for her life. One thing about me was I had come to realize there were some folks who needed help but didn't want my or anybody's help. And I damn sure couldn't help someone who wasn't ready. It just wouldn't work, so I had learned to stay in my lane, even where my children were concerned. I swear the older I became, I was turning into my mother. I could hear her voice say plain as day, "There are the people who said they wanted your help but didn't think they needed it. Then there are the people who really needed your help but didn't want it. Then there are folks who didn't want help *yet* because they weren't actually ready, Then there are folks who simply wanted and needed help, but for whatever reason didn't want help from the person trying to help them. That said a lot. And like a lot of things my mother used to say, I didn't understand, but I do now.

Basically, like I said, I've learned not to waste my time trying to help someone who isn't willing to do what it takes to help themselves. And again, that included my children, so most of the times when they reached out to me with their urgent need for help, I pretty much offered a listening ear and on occasion some recommendations or alternative solutions for them to consider how they might resolve whatever challenge they were facing, and I left it for them to figure out their best solution. I found it was better that way, for them and most importantly for me.

Hell, there was no point in me stressing myself out. In the end, they'd wind up doing what they wanted to do anyhow, no matter what I said or thought about it. In my mind, I wished them the best and moved on.

CHAPTER 16

For some time now, I had been thinking about doing something different with my hair, especially since I hadn't been able to get an appointment with my African hair braider to have my faux locs redone, but I couldn't decide what I wanted. During one of my rare and infrequent phone chats with one of my traveling girlfriends Suni, I'd ask her what she thought about me going naturally gray.

"Well, girlfriend, you know I'm older than you, so I ain't trying to look no older than my sixty-nine-year-old ass is already. Besides, I love the creativity of the African American women culture, especially as it relates to our hair. I mean, one day our hair is red, the next day it's yellow, the next day it's blonde, or whatever. I like that. Spoken like a true hair connoisseur," Suni said.

My friend didn't hesitate to change her hair however she wanted to. We were chumping at the bit on the phone as we occasionally would do to catch up to stay connected as often as reasonably achievable like good long-distance friends do.

"Yeah, definitely to each his or her own. As they say, everything ain't for everybody. But it's funny you mentioned the hair color thing 'cause for women our age, it's sort of hard attracting a decent man when you're sporting too extreme of a hair color. But Suni girl, you have always been bold with the hair colors—blondes and red hairstyles. That has always been one of the things I've most admired about you. No one can pull off some of the styles you wear but you. I think it's a whole look as well as personality. Besides, you've always been bold and vivacious," I said. "And speaking of attracting a man, have you met a man yet that you might even possibly be interested in?"

I thought I'd slide that question in out of nowhere to try to catch Suni off guard. Knowing as soon as I said it that Suni, being the sharp tongued, quick-witted person she was, nothing usually caught her off guard. That girl always had a clever comeback. If anything, we usually had to brace ourselves for what she was about to say.

"Girl, what's that? Like I tell anybody who asks me about a love life, it's been so long, when I do finally get one, I want a young one. I just want to flick that thang back and forth, girl. He's gonna think, *What's wrong with this old-ass woman?* I just want to lay there and flick it back and forth. He ain't even got to put it in, girl. Just let me lie there and let me play wit' it," Suni said for a shock factor. By her response, I knew I had set my own self up.

We both laughed, then I said to Suni, "Girl, I know that's right! Same here. Except for me, I want to do more than just flick that thang, and that's all I'mma say." We giggled some more. I could always count on Suni for a good laugh.

"*Umm-hmm.* Well, that's all I wanna do, girl. Remember when you asked me if at my age I still think about sex? I answered, 'Hell yeah, I do, and I still do,'" Suni said.

"Yes, I remember, and I also recall you telling me how afraid you were that your stuff was gonna dry up from no use too," I replied, still giggling.

"Real talk, friend. You have got to keep yourself lubricated and stimulated, otherwise your shit will dry up. What do you think happens to athletes? Hell, our bodies are no different. Men and women are alike in that regard. What do they say, if you don't use it, you lose it? Back to athletes, they work out to be in the best physical shape to run track, play whatever sport, and they are muscular, toned, and firm. Well, guess what happens when they stop participating in the sport if they don't continue their physical routines? Hell, I'll tell you what happens: Their asses get out of shape—and quickly. Remember if you don't use it, you lose it," Suni said.

"Girl, that's a scary thought, but you know what? I believe you're right. Hell, so what does a girl do? I mean I have some toys and things, but I will admit I haven't used them lately," I said barely audible as if having made a confession.

"Well, you'd better damn sure make it part of your self-care regimen and use them muthafuckas 'cuz as I always say, you stay ready so you ain't gotta get ready. So with that thought in mind, you better add self-stimulation to the damn list, boo. Real talk, girlfriend, real talk," Suni said.

"Suni, you are crazy as hell, girl. I don't know what we're going to do with you," I said.

"Nah, the better question is what would y'all asses do without me schoolin' you? See, Harmony and Connie got a man. We don't. You and Fav are not married, so you're still single as far as I'm concerned, so you and me gotta stay on top of thangs."

"Okay, yeah girl, I guess you've made your point. You might just be right about that," I reluctantly gave in and said to Suni.

"I know damn well I'm right, hell you betta get with the program. Otherwise, you're gonna find your ass out in the cold. Bria, you are a grown-ass woman. Some things you should already know. Get yourself a boy toy and handle your business, I'm good. I am sixty-nine years old. This young thang I have is twenty-nine years younger than me, and I am having the time of my life," Suni laughed loudly and exclaimed.

"Suni, are you freakin' kidding me? That's you. I'll pass on the boy toy for now, I'm good. Now, don't get me wrong, I'm not opposed to a younger man, but at the same time, I don't want to roll over and face some man-child who reminds me of my son," I said, literally shaking my head. I had heard it all.

"Yeah, okay, that's what your mouth say. But I'm not the one walking around here all uptight and shit worrying about and managing my grown-ass kids' lives either, now am I? Life is too short for that. When's the last time you had a good oil change? And I ain't talkin' 'bout on that damn Audi. I'm talkin' 'bout you? Don't even bother answering, I already know. It's been a minute 'cause I ain't heard nothing about Fav being in town. And if Connie and Harmony knew something, they didn't tell my black ass. Then again, your secretive ass wouldn't have mentioned it anyway. Am I right about that too?" Suni said as she finally took a breath and paused for my response as if she'd had a matter-of-fact revelation.

I didn't bother answering because she was right. Over the course of our friendship, we talked about a lot of things, but at the end of the day, the girlfriends didn't need to know everything about my business. In my mind, one thing Suni had said struck a chord with me, the part about me being too consumed with managing my adult children's lives, now those words left me something to process.

CHAPTER 17

I was rereading my journal and was going over some passages I'd written about our travels to South Africa. I seemed to have become transfixed by a wave of emotion. I closed my eyes and thought about our first stop being in London, how it felt traveling aboard the plane with all the people; the arrival, the hustle and bustle through the airport to the Heathrow Station, the touring of the London Eye, actually seeing Buckingham Palace and Westminster Abbey, walking through the parks, getting coffee and chocolates in Soho. It was like my mind was doing an instant replay of the most memorable experience I'd had to date. And to think no one was thinking about a virus or anyone being contagious. How different the times were. Would we ever go back to that?

Man, how I was getting cabin fever and ready to catch a plane to somewhere, anywhere. Being cooped up was not where it was at. I will never take for granted what a luxury it is to be able to travel abroad.

Over in the night, I got up to use the bathroom and woke up to find I had fallen asleep in my clothes. Out of habit, I reached over on my nightstand for my glasses so I could look at my phone display to see the time when I noticed I had a couple of missed call notifications from Zach. Then I saw a text message, *wyd,* which was text lingo for what are you doing, then another one read, *give me call. I need to talk to you about something.* Even though the pages of the calendar turned from February 2020 to our present time in 2021, Zach and I hadn't had a good one-on-one since the spectacle he'd made of himself at my birthday event. Despite the passage of time, I knew there were unspoken words and unresolved emotions that needed to be dealt with. I knew Zach rarely called out of the blue saying he needed to talk. So, I figured this was an opportunity for me to have the conversation that was still desperately needed. Instinctively, the next thing I thought was there must have been some life-or-death urgency thing going on. I sat straight up in my bed and reread his text message and immediately felt sick to my stomach for missing his call. *That's what I get for putting my phone on silent.* I had the tendency to do that when I knew I needed a night of uninterrupted sleep and so I wouldn't be disturbed by social media notifications and other phone disturbances. Without any further hesitation, I hit the video app icon on my phone to return Zach's call.

"What's up, Mom?" Zach responded.

"What's up? Are you kidding me? You called me. I'm returning your call. Are you okay?"

"Oh yeah, I did text you. I almost forgot. So, get this, I got a call from this chick I used to deal with back in the day. First, she was asking me if I remembered her. I didn't recognize the number, and I didn't recognize the voice, so I thought it was just somebody playing on my phone. Well anyway, let me get straight to it. How 'bout it was that girl that used to come by the house when me and Jason was in high school," Zach said.

"What girl are you referring to, Zach? There was so many," I said.

"You know the girl, Mom. Her sister was an extra in that John Singleton movie and was trying to be an actress," Zach said.

"Oh, yeah. Now I remember. Yeah, I guess I know who you're talking about. So how is this important to me, Zach? What's this about?" I said, getting irritated and ready to undress so I could get in bed now that I knew no one was dead or no one's house was on fire.

"Well, anyhow she says to me, 'So you gonna act like you don't know me now? Oh, okay. Funny it wasn't like that when I lost my virginity to you when you graduated high school.' I said, 'What are you talking about? Who is this? And when and where? I need to know this is not a joke.' She went on to describe the whole situation, and I realized who it was. Honestly, I had already kind of figured out who she was, but I was kind of playing it off."

"Everything is not a joking matter, honey. So go on. Then what did she say?" I asked.

"Just listen. I'mma get to it. See, Jason had gotten with her sister, and I was kicking it with her. I know, Mom, this might be too much information for you, but you know we can talk about anything," Zach said.

"Or so y'all think y'all can talk to me about anything," I said under my breath.

"Whatever. You know we tell you everything," Zach said.

"Boy, go on before I hang up this phone," I said.

"So, we went upstairs into my room when we lived, you know, in the house on the west side in Rockford. Well, that's all the detail I need to give you for now." Zach chuckled before he continued his story. "Well, after all these years, come to find out this girl is telling me she had a kid, and she's telling me the kid is mine."

I shot up to my feet as if I'd been hit by a bolt of lightning.

"Zach, let me tell you something. I don't know if that's a possibility or not, but I will say this: Before you go jumping on anybody's bandwagon claiming a kid and believing them telling you that child is yours after all these years, you had better do your due diligence and get a DNA test done. The way it is these days, these young ladies go out saying a certain guy is the father of their child. They get the families all involved, and come to find out, these kids are not even theirs. I don't know what you intend to do about this situation. Clearly that's something you need to figure out—and sooner rather than later.

"I swear men and their damn penises. It never fails to amaze me. So, get yourself together. I hope you're not drinking. Do whatever it is you need to do and contact that young lady back ASAP!"

And just like that, I had lost it on Zach. All my therapy out the window, I had relapsed. I felt my blood pressure boiling. My body temperature was hot, and I could feel my hand sweating.

"*Awww*, man, here you go. How come it's got to be something as serious as that?" Zach asked.

"Man, snap out of it. What the hell else can it be? A whole child? Are you seriously asking that question? Let's be for real, Zach. Everything's not a joke. Why would a woman reach out to a man after twenty-something years to tell him he's a father? It's very likely true. Hell, back in those days, you and Jason were slinging it so hard it's wonder you don't have a whole tribe running around town. Damn. No judgment from me—but then again a lot of judgment from me. I'm your mother. Who better to tell you than me? But now, you're a grown-ass man, so you need to deal with that issue and figure it out. I hope I'm wrong, but highly unlikely," I said.

"Yeah, I know, and you're usually never wrong," Zach said.

"Oh, and one more question, was the sex consensual?" I asked.

"Now, why would you ask that, Mom? Why would you even think that I would be in any situation other than consensual? But to your question, yes definitely, always Mom. I would never force my way on anyone," Zach said.

"I'm just asking because you know that's a whole other issue and an entirely different conversation. Look at what happened to Bill Cosby. You know I had to ask. I was just hoping and praying that it wasn't anything like that."

"Man, Mom, I just can't with you," Zach said.

"Boy, I'm like your damn attorney. You better come clean with me so I know how to help your ass. I'm just saying call me when you know more. Love you," I said.

"I love you too, Mom," Zach said.

CHAPTER 18

I knew I had relapsed big time after speaking with my son. Sometimes it be your own family who gaslights you and sets you off. No matter how hard I tried to stay on course, someone came along and knocked me smooth off gear. I felt like the family member of an alcoholic, which by the way I am, who needed an Al-Anon meeting. Strange how that thought occurred in my mind. I grabbed my journal to write, and I was distracted as I read what I had written weeks ago recapping one of my therapy sessions: *Today the topic came up that some women received mixed messages from men and developed false narratives from these scenarios due to a lack of communication. I had been pondering that stance and come to know that by choice, I had been one of those women. For example, Fav and I had been casual sex partners for several years. As with all matters of the heart, I had a difficult time keeping my emotions intact. When the relationship began, it was mutually assumed there would be no strings attached. Fav seemed to be okay with our arrangement for so much of that time, and it went without saying that our*

relationship remained the same with no changes. I, on the other hand, longed to go to the next level. I thought I wanted exclusivity.

So, in my mind, to keep the relationship, I never let him know my desires. Truth be told, I wasn't ready then. What I've come to know is I'd been an emotional mess. I carried too much baggage, and I am not referring to my children, not at all. The baggage I'm referring to was due to my past unmet emotional needs. I suffered from dysfunctional communication skills in relationships, I retreated upon confrontation, I put up a superficial wall to protect myself against hurt and betrayal, even when there was no real evidence of betrayal present. I had poor boundaries and lashed out when my needs weren't met. I thought I knew my worth. I didn't. I felt I wasn't good enough, so I put the needs of others first.

I breathe a sigh of relief to know I've learned the value of delayed gratification through self-regulation and self-control. I can see clearly now. I know me, my value, and my worth. I've learned anything worth having is worth taking the time to work for. I'm worth fighting for, and as I evolved, I give myself grace. I'm a work in progress in a process. I've learned to respect the process and my journey.

After reading and then re-reading that passage, I knew I was okay and not to be so hard on myself for letting off some steam with Zach. I'm only human; I will make mistakes even as I continued to heal. That's what this thing life is all about. That's the beauty of journaling too. There are times I need to be reminded that life won't ever be perfect, and neither is family.

Things come up all the time; they always will. The difference is knowing how to manage things and to not let life's obstacles manage me. I released it. That was Zach's issue to deal with, not mine. I intentionally shifted my mind to me and my present. My son would be alright. I heard myself say out loud. "*Hmmm.* I wonder what I should have to eat today. Alexa, play songs by Anita Baker."

"Anita Baker songs from Apple Music'" was Alexa's reply, and the music started playing.

Journaling had been a gift and a curse. I did it because I believe it was an outlet for me to privately release my thoughts, emotions, and feelings in a safe and private place. I found it therapeutic to release all of my pent-up emotions freely. But at times, I found it difficult to re-read what I'd written. I don't know if it was the transparency aspect of it or seeing in context my vulnerabilities that was hard for me to come face to face with.

I made myself do it despite my anxiety sometimes because I knew I needed the honest self-reflection. I needed to know what areas of my life I'd been redundant in and what things I needed to change to evolve. Lord knows I appreciated evolvement.

Over time, journaling worked for me. I knew I didn't always have exceptional communication skills or what it took in interpersonal relationships, but I did know how to write my feelings out. I chuckled at this thought because I thought about a time from my youth when there was a boy I liked at school and I would write him small notes and pass them to my best friend to give to him. Life was so simple then, but guess what? You can't write notes to people now. This is real life. You must own your feelings. I'm not that little girl anymore. I've learned to set boundaries for myself, hold myself accountable, and set goals by staying organized and motivated.

I put my pen aside, closed my journal, and decided to go to my fridge. I poured a nice, chilled glass of Prosecco. I retreated to my room, set the glass on a mirrored coaster atop my nightstand, and crawled into my plush bedding covers with several pillows propped behind my back for support. I reached for the glass, leaned backed, inhaled, exhaled, took a sip, smiled, and thought, *I've had an amazing journey and despite all my shortcomings, there's still grace. I'm worthy of it.* At that moment, I was reminded of a Bible passage about new mercies, meaning as long as I have breath in my body, I have a chance to get better.

CHAPTER 19

March 2021

It's as if I looked up, figuratively speaking, and *poof!* The year 2020 had been all a blur. It was as if we had all been living in a fog or stuck in some sort of abyss in time from another space. Being shut off from people and not being able to move about freely, who would ever thunk it as they say, that life as we knew it would come to a screeching halt literally.

It was hard to imagine that life, seeing all the traffic on the roads as I drove along. Things were gradually getting back to normal. Maysa and the ladies at Diva's were back up and running. The malls had reopened but had acquired a new close time of eight p.m., and the churches were back in face-to-face service. I was getting all my dentist, doctor, and ophthalmologist appointments scheduled on time but with a requirement to wear a mask. I'd gotten acclimated to our new normal without a fight. I didn't have a choice.

It was surreal. I'd opted to get the COVID-19 vaccinations in Fair Park in Dallas as soon as the opportunity became available to my age group, and I'd recommended for Zach, India, and Shea to do so in Illinois as well as anyone they knew or would be in contact with. All vaxed up, that would be a constant part of our convo. I couldn't make an appointment with any medical facility without first completing a questionnaire regarding whether I'd had a fever, flulike symptoms, or experienced a headache or nausea. At every public place I visited, the businesses' entrances had dispensers filled with sanitary wipes and disposable masks. Everyone was on board with taking whatever precautionary measures were needed to remain healthy—well, almost everyone. There were a few conspiracy theorists folks who believed the government was infringing on their rights. Some of them didn't even believe the virus was a real phenomenon. But for me, it was clear COVID-19 was the new plague, and for the most part, no one in their right mind wanted to get it.

As if COVID-19 wasn't enough to deal with, I didn't know what was going on with people. It seemed everybody I talked to was having some sort of mental health issue going on. While out on my usual Target run, India called and wanted to know if I had spoken with Zach. My reply was no I had not.

"At least not since we talked last week, but when I talked with him, he seemed like he had a lot of issues going on," I said, not wanting to disclose what Zach had told me about the possible child.

"Well, I was just wondering 'cause Shea said, from what she could piece together from the last time he was by her place, it sounded like he and Samantha broke up—again. He was at Shea's apartment drunk again, and it was in the middle of the day. If I know my brother as well as I know I do, he did something to cause that girl to leave his butt alone. He *stay* messing up. I dunno what's wrong with him," India said.

"Not...what's wrong with him. It's what happened to him is what I'd like to know," I said, thinking out loud.

India either didn't hear me or disregarded what I said as she went on with her rant about Zach.

"Oh, well, invariably that's his M.O., and how he chooses to handle things when things don't go his way is on him. I'm done-done with trying to figure out other so-called grown people's lives, Mom. Zach needs to take accountability for his dumb behavior. It's too much. I don't know how that young lady kept putting up with his mess for as long as she did anyway. I guess he'll figure it out one day." India was going a mile a minute. I almost couldn't get a word in edgewise.

"I hope so," was all I had left in me to say.

I was so ready to get off the phone with her. I was tired of hearing about the situation with Zach and most of all tired of the rift between my children.

"Yeah, well, I didn't mean to get you all riled up. I was just asking," India said.

One thing I will say is I will not make excuses for my son's behavior. I've tried to be there for him, but Zach refused to share his true feelings with me. And since I'm not a mind reader, I had no way of knowing what things were bothering him now or from his past. I'd wondered for years what made him act out the way he does. We've all sat on the sidelines and witnessed how he'd lost several good relationships in the past.

I could feel my blood pressure boiling, and I started twirling my faux locs from underneath my head wrap, a sure sign I was being agitated as twirling my fingers in my hair had always been a nervous habit of mine. I knew if it was true what India was telling me about Samantha, then this was no different than before. Damn, just as I was thinking about Zach, I wondered if he hadn't gotten that particular behavior pattern from me in some weird sort of way. Not to make it about me, but there had been some similarities. The difference with me was that I was in therapy. He wasn't. I think Zach was like a lot of other Black men who thought all therapy entailed was telling another person all your business and them judging you for the things you shared. I made a mental note to call Zach later that night.

I know all the talk about how I shouldn't blame myself for my grown children's behavior, but now that I know better, I dropped the ball. I provided for them physically, but I didn't have the emotional capacity to give them what they needed when I reared them. I needed to let them know that I had to be honest about it. There wasn't anything I could do to undo what had already been done, but I couldn't live another day without having an honest conversation with them to let them know.

"Can you believe it's June already, girl? I see these folks walking around here with no masks and shit, but I'm still wearing mine. I'm not playing. This stuff is too serious," Maysa said.

"Yeah. It's still COVID-19 as far as I'm concerned too. I'm glad I live alone. I don't have to worry about social distancing too much since I'm by myself. I worry about my kids though. You know it's hard for young people to stay still. I'm just glad no one in my family has had it yet," I said.

"You're right. I had to snatch Olivia's tail about going so much. My niece act like she doesn't get how serious this thing is," Maysa said.

"She's young. It's hard for them to be away from their friends and stuff like that. You remember how it was when you were young? The young people of today are no different. But as long as I have my phone and can connect virtually, I'm cool," I said.

"I'm glad business is picking up. It was a challenge, but we were able to get some of that emergency funding from the government, so we were able to keep Diva's afloat," Maysa said.

"You all were blessed in that regard. Not everyone was that fortunate. I've heard so many small businesses didn't make it. Hell, some churches didn't make it. I'm glad you ladies are hanging in there though. Girl, let me take this call. It's Shea. Let me see what she wants. I'll call you later," I said.

"Mom, where are you?" I heard a different sounding Shea on the other end of the phone and automatically put my right hand over my heart as if to keep it intact. It was the sound that was about to be said next I had to be braced for.

"I'm home. What's going on? Are you okay?" I asked.

"*Ummm,* yeah, I am, but it's Zach. He's alive—"

"He's alive. What is it, Shea?"

"Apparently Zach fell asleep at the wheel while driving in his car. he. From what I was told, his car went into a ditch on Bypass Twenty." Initially, I could tell by the shakiness in Shea's voice that she was hesitant and anxious to deliver this news to me. But once she got it out, I felt her relief to have that weight lifted.

"Where is he, Shea, and is he okay?" I asked, trying with everything in me to remain calm because I didn't want to upset Shea any more than I knew she was already. It was all I could do to hold myself together though.

"Yes. Actually, he's fine, Mom. Samantha called me and told me. They didn't want me to tell you because Zach knew you'd be tripping, but I said I was going to tell you anyway. And he's lucky because his car is okay too. But just so you know, he had been drinking."

That was all I needed to hear. As soon as Shea said Zach was fine, I was furious. I couldn't put off talking to Zach any longer. One thing I knew about Shea, she was not the one to hold secrets too well in our family. She had always been that way, even as a child. My mother used to say, "That baby Shea gon' sing like a bird, so don't tell her nothing you don't want anyone to know."

Zach and India would get so upset with Shea for telling on them and would terrorize her when she was a little girl. It would mainly be India doing the bullying. She would do stuff like locking Shea out of her room or not sharing toys and things like that, nothing real serious, but it used to hurt my baby Shea's feelings so much. Shea would come crying to me about how bad India treated her sometimes, and I would just tell her what a kind and sweet person she was and not to let anyone change her. My words would comfort her, and she'd go running straight back to India to try to win her over. Those were the good days—the days when I had my babies, all of them under one roof, and I could protect them. I shook my head as I thought about the good times we did have as a family. Thank God, it wasn't all bad for us back then.

At least I didn't think it was. As soon as I got off the phone with Shea, I hit my call log with Zach's number. My call went straight to voicemail. Immediately I knew what that meant. Zach must have been hitting that reject button, which was a tactic folks did to people they didn't want to talk to. What kind of person rejects their mother's call? Zach knew me like a book though. I knew that once he found out that I'd heard about his latest debacle, he wouldn't want to hear what I'd have to say about it. And no doubt he wasn't wrong. I felt like I was at my wit's end with him, and I intended to let him know.

I fell into a complete rage when I began speaking to the voicemail like a frantic lunatic. "Zach, I know you see me calling. Now if you don't pick up this damn phone right now! Have you completely lost your mind? What are you going to do? Are you going to keep on 'til you kill somebody! Are you nuts?" By the last episode of my calling Zach's phone and my calls going to voicemail, my voice had raised, I grew more tense, and I was pointing my finger in the air, and no one was listening. Finally, when I came to myself, I threw up my fists in the air and screamed as loud as I could. I wiped at the tears streaming down my face out of frustration and yelled, "Damn, damn, damn."

I was angry and disappointed in Zach, but I was more disappointed in myself for how enraptured I'd become in a situation that had nothing to do with me. Here I sat an emotional wreck, and my son was likely somewhere totally unbothered. Now what sense did that make?

CHAPTER 20

J ust as I suspected, Shea couldn't hold water, and she told India all about the incident with Zach. Like clockwork, India was blowing my phone up. It's not like they don't all live in Rockford. Stuff goes on right where they are, and instead of them rallying together to figure things out first, they reach out to me as if I am the Queen of England.

"I told Shea that she shouldn't even bother checking on him. He's got to figure it out. What's his problem? Does he know how lucky he is? That could have gone all bad," India ranted.

I swear if I didn't know better, I would've thought she was my eldest child and not Zach. She could be quite the worrier of the three of them. She would always say to me, "I am the eldest. I can't help it that you had your eldest child second."

And I would say, "Whatever, India."

Anyhow, at this point, I was so outdone, I could barely get a word in. For someone who didn't want to be bothered, she sure wasn't acting like it.

"Yeah, well you know how kindhearted Shea is. The last thing she'll do is not see about anybody she loves when they're going through something, especially Zach. She's always been like that." I sighed, then said, "I tried calling his ass, but he wouldn't take my calls, and I was about to ring him again, but you called first. As soon as we're done, I need to try and get through to him. I can't let this go. Like you said, we would be having a totally different conversation had things gone another way. I don't even want to think about it. Zach needs some help. This is getting way out of hand, and I won't feel comfortable with myself if I don't make another attempt to reach him. I suppose that's what I get for being his mother. You know what I mean. A mother is the last person to give up on their child," I said as I mentally prepared myself for what approach to use with Zach this time around.

"Well, I guess…" India said.

"Honey, I know. Just pray Zora never puts you through any drama. Better yet, keep living. You'll see," I said assuredly.

Some people tend to say once a parent has raised their children, they've done their due diligence and their children are on their own to fend for themselves. I disagree with that theory. I believe the constructs of the adult child and parent changes, but I'm no less a parent because the child is an adult. We go from raising our children when they are young to advisers when they are adults—at least that's how I see it.

I've always had to fend for myself. Except for the sporadic guidance I received from a friend's parent, or as I got older, my girlfriends, it's been trial by error for me. I wasn't going to inflict that on my own children. I plan to be there for them as a consultant or guidance counselor. At least then, I knew they had the proper tools to ultimately figure things out on their own. That for me was my due diligence.

I had been trying to reach Zach for weeks. He was still refusing my calls and ignoring my texts. In the meantime, Shea contacted me again and said he was ashamed and wasn't ready to talk to me yet. I figured he'd call me when he got ready. I'd had some time to think about what I was going to say to him the next time around, minus all the yelling and cussing. It helped that I'd had a therapy session since my emotional last outburst on his voicemails, which I referred to as my relapse. I discussed the Zach incident with my therapist during my entire session because I was looking for some solace as to how I lost it.

With time and a good therapy session, I had calmed down tremendously. My therapist reiterated how proud of me she was, that I owned my shortcomings and she stated I should give myself some grace. She agreed that I could be a bit too absorbed in managing my son's life and more than likely had lost my balance. She asked me to consider allowing him—them for that matter, Shea and India as well—to make their own decisions. She stated I should trust that I had raised them well, even if they make mistakes. That's how they learn and grow. All of which I knew and thought I was doing when all it took was one major setback for me and bam, just like that, I was back like I didn't know any better. I suppose I needed an outsider to shake my ass back into my recovery zone. Then, of course, she gave me another homework assignment. She asked me to think about what I could have done different in my handling of the situation.

I guess it was a good thing Zach hadn't taken my call during my rage. I'm sure I would've been sorry for a lot worse than the tantrums I did throw on the voicemail. In a way, that was a win for him and showed growth on his part for not having any interaction with a mother who was seemingly out of control.

I'm not giving him a pass for his behavior either. It's just that I'm not trying to be the person I'd been in the past. All the belligerent, berating, and manipulative immature parenting was swept away. I decided I would offer a healthy and supportive role to him when he was ready for me to.

For the time being, I jotted down a few things to do, I was going to respect all of their boundaries, or at least try, 'cause I'm still a work in progress. I can focus more on self-care by prioritizing my own well-being. Maybe even find a hobby or some other thing that interested me to find some fulfillment outside my children's lives. I might even check into Top Golf, pickle ball, or axe throwing, which sounded like fun and stress relieving. Yeah, that's it. I needed a hobby.

CHAPTER 21

I didn't know how to approach it, but I knew it was time to address the shift in the relationship between Connie, Harmony, Suni and I. I didn't know if our issues had to do with the pulling apart of our lives due to the stress from the pandemic or what was happening, but something just didn't feel right and I knew it had to change..

I was sharing my thoughts with Maysa. "To my knowledge, I haven't done anything or said anything about anybody. Oh, Connie and I did have a difference of opinion about that sou-sou or board shit she tried to get me in. That's all I could think of. Other than that, I'm just not going to worry about it. Suni and I still talked regularly. She's crazy as hell. She doesn't give a damn about any bullshit. Besides, Suni has never been one to bite her tongue. When something is off with one of us, she's always been the one to step in and address it," I said as I was going over in my mind trying to find a cause for the dissension I felt.

"I get it. Sometimes people grow apart for whatever reason. You ladies have been friends for so long though. Just give it some time. Some things work themselves out. You can never go wrong by asking though, if it's something that's really bothering you. You never know what could be going on. And it's Harmony and Connie who are married, right?" Maysa said.

"Right. I thought about that too. It could be that they're just dealing with their own personal home issues with their spouses and family. Besides, they both have adult children and grandchildren, too, so who knows what it could be. And to your point about me saying something if it's bothering me that bad, well right now, it's not because I have more pressing issues going on with my own immediate family. Right now, I'm more concerned with the mental health of what I've got going on ova here, if you get what I'm saying. Anyway, that's that. Enough about me. What's been going on with you? You said you had something you wanted to talk with me about. I have time. What is it?" I spoke.

"Are you sure you have time, girl? 'Cause this shit is so heavy I don't know who else to talk to," Maysa said.

She sounded like she had lost all her enthusiasm. This was not the energetic, vibrant, pick-me-up, always encouraging woman I was used to talking to. I could tell something was weighing heavy on my friend's mind.

"Yes, I do. What is it?" I asked, preparing myself for the worst and making sure my background noises were nil. I knew in my heart that whatever Maysa needed to share didn't need any distractions.

"So, let me give it to you straight no chaser. For starters, you know Olivia, my niece. Well…she's not my niece. She's my daughter," Maysa said.

"Oh my God, really? Does she know? Does anyone else know?" I asked before even thinking I might be asking too many questions too fast.

"No. Olivia doesn't know. Isla and Mona are the only ones I've ever trusted enough to share my family secret with. This is what happened…I just don't know where to begin…how to say this other than to come on out and say it. When I was about thirteen, I was raped by my brother, not the one we told Olivia was her father, but my older brother. He lived with us at the time when we lived in a very small town in back woods Texas. In those days, we didn't have much. All the kids played together, and there would be this game called playing house or you're the momma, I'm the daddy. Well, needless to say, I've always been overdeveloped for my age, so of course my older brother and I were always the 'the momma and daddy.'" Maysa used air quotes to describe the pretend relationship.

I knew the instant when he had gone too far when he penetrated me. I felt sick to my stomach. I tried to push him off me, but he wouldn't stop. He just kept going until I guess he had reached his point of no return. I was so ashamed. For a long time, I wouldn't talk or play with any of the kids. It was my mother who finally noticed something was wrong with me. She shook the truth out of me but made me promise never to mention what happened to anyone, especially not our father because Momma knew he would kill my brother. I had always been a daddy's girl, and Momma knew my dad would protect me even though she did not," Maysa said with a mixture of distress, fear, and humility.

"Maysa, I'm so sorry you had to go through that," I said, not knowing what else to say to my friend. My heart sank as she shared more details.

"Momma conjured up a whole story that I had been raped by a young man at the local convenience store. She said we couldn't go to the police because it would bring shame to our family. I was too young to know better, so instead of telling the truth, I went with Momma's story. I went with that story so long that I had started to believe that it was the truth and that anything different I said would only make it look like I had caused what happened to me," Maysa said.

"Honey, let me tell you, you're not the reason that happened to you, and you have nothing to be ashamed of," I said.

"It's taken me quite some time to know that now. Anyhow, knowing how backward the folks were in the small town we lived in then, I just know I would have been cast as a whore. It would have been my fault. Nothing in me makes me believe that wouldn't have been the case. Well, fast forward, our family moved to Waxahachie, and by that time, my older brother was dealing with his own demons, and he had left home. Last we all knew, he joined the railroad or some shit. I don't really know or care what happened to him. After we moved and I gave birth to Olivia, one look at her, and I knew I had to protect my child. My mother didn't protect me, my brother violated me, so there was no way I was going to let this innocent child live with the threat of something like that ever happening to her. It was Daddy who came up with the idea that we say Olivia was my niece and that her biological father had run off with his crack head girlfriend, who was said to be her mother. Because Olivia has been taught about the effects of drug abuse, she never questioned our story. Neither did she want to get to know either of her biological parents because we gave her so much love and affection. The painful thing is sometimes I look in Olivia's eyes, and I see my brother. That's a lot to deal with, even now."

"It must be painful for you to relive this story and share it with me. I'm proud of your strength. That takes a lot of courage," I finally managed to say.

"Yeah, well, the part I need help with is now, after all these years, that vile nigga has been trying to reach out to Momma 'cause he knows how weak minded she is with Daddy being gone now to try to find out if his name is listed in their will. You know, Momma got COVID-19 a while ago, and truth be told, she hasn't quite been the same since. Due to her age and other health ailments, I can see her wasting away. Honestly, I believe it's a matter of time before she transitions. That nigga got wind of it, and now he feels entitled to his equal share of whatever our parents have. I'm so pissed. I just can't believe that nigga's audacity. How dare he come back in the picture after all he's done?" Maysa declared, exasperated.

"Legally, he does have a right. It's rotten of him to ask for it, but he is your mother's son and just as entitled as you and your other siblings, unless…" I said as I got an idea.

"Unless what? If you have any ideas, I need to hear them—and now," Maysa said.

"Unless you put your big girl panties on and tell your brother unequivocally that you will let it be known publicly and take his ass to the authorities. Get an attorney and have his ass sign over any inheritance he might get. It's time out for that bullying. I don't care if he is your brother. He needs to be held accountable for what he did to you. And as far as Olivia goes, you'd be surprised at what people can handle when you're being honest with them. Truth always prevails, no matter how hard. Maysa, I believe you should consider not giving him any more power over your life than what he already has had. Enough is enough," I said.

"He is using this as a pawn over me, that's for damn sure. He has been threatening me to let it all out that he is Olivia's biological father…I just don't know what to do. I'm just so frustrated right now. I just don't know…I've been an emotional wreck about this entire thing for the past few weeks."

"Maysa! Damnit! Did you hear anything I just said? Shut the fuck up," I sighed and said after finally exhaling a long breath I'd been holding for what seemed like eternity as I tried to process all of what I was hearing.

"Huh? Girl, I was gone. Say it again. I'm just not thinking straight," Maysa said.

I hated to be so abrupt with my friend, but I needed to get her attention. And sometimes with Maysa, I have to give it to her in the raw. That's the only way she'll listen. Sometimes using a good, strong expletive puts a punch in a delivery statement to the point the receiver knows full and well that what was just said was meant for real and not for play. I repeated what I said about going to the police now, and I also said, "I don't know if there's any statute of limitation on rape, but his ass could go to jail for the fact that he raped you."

It took some persuading before it sunk in with Maysa, then she said, "Yeah, I know Miss Bria, but the thing is, I don't want to do that. I guess I could threaten to do that with him. I could tell him it's either he does that, or he could just leave, or I could threaten him with filing charges against him. But who would believe me? It would be my word against his. And as for that matter, let's just say he does get arrested. What about the whole process? This shit could drag on and on—our whole family business in the court system, more shame and embarrassment for me as well as Olivia—and I just don't want that to happen," Maysa said.

"Honey, that's my recommendation, and Lord knows I'm no expert on family matters. My family has enough of our own, but what I said is worth giving some thought to," I said, now damn near emotionally exhausted myself. I could only imagine the load all of this had been on Maysa.

"So, you see there's always something going on. When you think your family is dysfunctional, there's someone always worse," Maysa said.

"Sho' you're right, and the last time I checked, there's not a Richter scale I know of that measures family dysfunction. All families have some form of dysfunction is the way I see it. So, it's not a matter of whose is worse. It's like ice cream—it's all the same, just many different flavors.

Maysa was right. What she shared with me was a lot to unpack. I felt so bad that she had to carry that load for so long by herself. I had to remind myself that her story wasn't my battle, and I needed to resist the urge to want to fix it for her. And although I knew her thing wasn't for me to fix, the next words I heard out of my mouth was, "I just wish there was something I could do to make you feel better, but I just want you to know I love you, and I'm here for you. If there's anything that you need from me emotionally, just say the word, and I'm there for you. I also want you to know this is safe place for you, with me I mean. I'm no longer the quicker picker-upper, but you can place bets that you're in a safe place with me, and you can share anything with me. *Ummm*, it's not going anywhere, except for you, me, and the walls."

"Thank you so much. I appreciate you. I needed to let that go today. And yes, I have my pastor and a therapist, but right now, I needed to let someone know I'm not alright, and I needed to do that right now. Like I said, I've had mental therapy for years and especially with the help of my faith, my pastor, and our church and all that…otherwise there's no way I would have been able to keep my mind together," Maysa said.

"Sometimes I wonder if our ancestors know how traumatized we are from the shit they drilled into us like, *Do as I say, not as I do; what goes on in this house stays in this house;* and even that nonsense about loving a relative in spite of how they mistreat you," I said.

"The biggest lie I ever had to live by was, *That's still your mother, that's still your brother.* What? Are you fa real right now? Somebody must have forgotten to give them the loyalty memo 'cause how is it that we're supposed to excuse bad behavior, mistreatment, and even disrespect on the strength of a person being kinfolk?" Maysa asked.

"I know, girl, I know," I said, nodding in agreement. "Back in those days, I guess our parents went through so much, and they handled things so much differently than how things should be dealt with—upfront and not swept under the rug," I said compassionately.

"Yeah, 'cause there's so much shit hidden under the rug ova here that I feel like I need on hiking boots to get through the damn door," Maysa said.

"And I understand why you feel that way, 'cause that's a lot to deal with. The real issue is figuring out where to start. You've got to pull yourself together and come up with a strategy. *Hmmmph,* unfortunately, this won't be an easy fix. I honestly think this is something you will need professional support, I mean like a person who specializes in trauma and abuse. Maysa, this is serious. I'm also thinking you might need some legal assistance."

At first, I thought the phone line went dead. Maysa took a deep breath, causing a moment of silence in our conversation. Then as if a lightning bolt struck her I heard her say with courage, a mixture of determination, and vulnerability, "I never thought it would come to this but you're right. I can't do this alone. I'll consider seeking professional help and legal support. It's time to face this head-on."

CHAPTER 22

I was having a good day. I got up at my normal hour—six a.m.—went for a walk and took in the fresh morning air. It had been a few days since I last spoke with Maysa on the phone, but during that time, we managed to keep in touch via text messages to do daily check-ins to say things like *You good?* or *Hey, girl. Let me know if you need me.* As I thought about it, no news was good news—for the time being. I knew once a person unpacked as much as what Maysa had during our last talk, there was no sense in probing her any further. People generally shared what they needed to at a particular time, and I didn't want to come across as being nosey. Even though I had so many questions, I knew better than to be too intrusive. I had to trust my better instinct that if Maysa needed me, she'd let me know. The love and bond in our sisterhood was infallible. Maysa had a safe place with me as far as I was concerned.

I still hadn't been able to reach Zach yet. I was growing concerned about his well-being, but I refused to let it consume me to the point of being my old overbearing self. Like the situation with Maysa, I didn't want to bug him, so I let it be. Maysa and Zach's issues were different in circumstances but similar in nature. They each needed time to figure out how to resolve their own issues. Where my son was concerned, I told myself sometimes it's best to leave things as they are and not bring up issues that could cause further trouble and unrest—at least for now. It was no easy feat, and oftentimes I'd feel my motherly intuitiveness kick in to want to call him and take care of him, protect him, fix things for him like I used to do when he was a little boy, but I shrugged those urges off. I had to resist my old nature to be the superhero mom that I had grown accustomed to being—the person who always came to my children's rescue. I believed in my mind and heart I had emotionally handicapped them enough. With those thoughts, I was left with no choice. I had to face it. It was time for me to let go and allow them to do this thing called adulting on their own. Besides, Shea had been doing a decent job of keeping both India and I up to date with what was going on with Zach. And from what I understood, Zach was making some effort toward a resolution for his battles, self-inflicted conundrum, and he was feeling some remorse.

I knew in my heart of hearts that I wanted to be a different parent than what I experienced from my own parents. Therapy had helped me grow emotionally and had helped to improve my interpersonal relationships with my children—for that matter, people overall. Looking back at how I was as compared to now, I was really a dressed-up mess as my Bea would say. I felt a sense of accomplishment and satisfaction in that I'd reached a point of letting go of past shame and embarrassment from my own childhood. And even though I had relinquished the shame and blame, I still felt accountable to how my children had been reared by me. I didn't care what anyone said, as their mother, I was responsible for raising them. God gave them to me and had entrusted me with their well-being, and at any time when I was remiss in that, whether intentional or not, I needed to own it, and I wasn't going to be satisfied until I admitted I got some things wrong, I made many mistakes, and going forward, I wanted us to grow and heal from the past. And it wasn't just what I wanted but more importantly, what they needed from me as a parent to help them grow emotionally.

I had made up my mind to start with Zach. I reached for my phone from my countertop. He must have been reading my mind because as I looked at my phone, there was a notification coming through from my son that read:

Hey. Not looking for a response from you. Just let me say this, I apologize. I'm sorry…I think my behavior is tearing you down…pulling us apart. I know you don't like it when we're at odds with each other. I love you. I love India, Shea, and Zora. I'll fix it. It's got to stop, and I'm done FRFR. I apologize to you, and I'm gonna fix this. Believe me, this is the last day of any BS from me. I know it's not cool, and I know it's disappointing to you and hurting you. I heard it in your voice the last time we spoke. I promise you I'm going to make this right. Have a good day, Mom.

I love you. Please don't respond. Just let me do what I gotta do to handle this.

I breathed a sigh of relief as I finished reading the text, and without any further hesitation, I instinctively tapped the little phone icon in the video messages app to dial his number.

"Hello," I heard Zach answer. I saw a distorted image before realizing it wasn't Zach's face, then as I zeroed in on the phone screen, it made sense to me what I was seeing, and I recognized the familiar art piece. The artwork hung on the wall in the living room of Zach's apartment. It was one of the designs that India had picked out when she helped Zach decorate his place after his split with his wife, Lydia. That time had seemed so long ago. Zach had been so broken after the split from Lydia, we all had banded together to help him through that dark time in his life and had done as caring families do in those types of situations. India, Shea, and I got together and stood by his side. We never condoned his behavior then, and our stance remains unchanged. Despite that, we were there for him. It's funny how that artwork, like a trigger, uncovered memories from that chapter of our lives, transporting us back as if it were the very day it unfolded.

My mind also shifted back to when I received the call from Shea screaming in the phone saying she was about to catch a case. Once I got her calmed down, she informed me that Zach had phoned her for help to go and retrieve his belongings from outside on a curb in front of the home that he and Lydia had shared. Long story short, Lydia had had all she could take from Zach. He had been caught—again—cheating, and she threw all his belongings out. In summary, Lydia had demanded he leave in the dead of winter with no place to go, like he was a stray dog. The rest is history. I thought that would've taught my son a valuable lesson, but as time has shown, it had not.

"Hey. How've you been?" I asked as if I was talking to a friend I hadn't spoken to in a while rather than speaking to my own son. And without waiting for his response, because I could tell he must be feeling awkward, I said, "I got your message, and that's not the reason why I'm calling. I appreciate the apology, and I accept it." There was more idle silence, so I went on. "There's something I've been meaning to talk with you about...just hear me out." This time, I heard a sigh from Zach as if in a "here it comes."

"You know I've been giving it a lot of thought about *ummm* well...I've always tried to fix what I thought was wrong with you as if you were like a broken object or something, and I could make it all better and our lives would be perfect. I guess I was living in some sort of fantasy world still always wanting this perfect family. Well, the truth is this, I've realized that in life, not all things are perfect. That's part of the definition of life, things happen, good and bad, especially in families. As a parent—and I'm not making excuses for anything—I just need to make it clear to you why I've been how I am toward you as your mother, and I hope you understand me. Yes, I was young when I had you. I didn't know anything about being a parent, let alone raising a child at sixteen. I didn't know anything about that, and I'm sure there were times when I wasn't there for you emotionally—or maybe I didn't give you the emotional support that you needed. I thought I was doing a good job as a parent because I worked and provided for you financially. I gave you a roof over your head and food on the table and those sorts of things, and I thought that was all that was required.

"Well, as I've matured, I've learned some things, and I am not the same person. Now I realize there's so much more than just those *uh* materialistic type things that children need, and so I want you to know I dropped the ball. I'm sorry about that, but I'm here for you now. I want you to know if there's any emotional support you need from me, I'm here. Now…you know I'm not saying I'm gonna pay your bills. You know it's not about back pay or some sort of bad parent reparations I owe you."

We both laughed. I was glad to ease the tension, and I knew I had Zach's attention because now his face was in view, and I saw his eyes.

"No, before you go any further, Mom, let me stop you," he said. "You know how you have asked me in the past about whether I'd been molested in my childhood, well *ummm*…there was something that may have happened to me like some sort of molestation, and I kind of shrugged it off."

I could feel the tension in me building up again as I braced myself for what Zach was about to say next.

"But you know, I have been giving that a lot of thought, like why you would ask me a question about being sexually abused. But then I started thinking about how you would say you detected hidden aggressions in me. I thought, *What the hell is Mom talking about?* So, I asked a couple of my homeboys if they thought I had any hidden aggressions, and they said hell yeah, which made me think more about my behavior when I got alone..."

"Yeah, I was asking you those things because in my own therapy I've learned that there are residual effects on adults that when triggered adults act on and carry certain negative behaviors into our adult relationships from our adverse childhood experiences. Most times you're triggered by something you've forgotten or suppressed and don't even realize it, and that turns into aggressive behavior. In other words, you know that these certain bad things have happened to you as a child, it becomes a hidden aggression when you pass it off. You don't want to deal with it, or maybe you just don't have the mental capacity to deal with it. You just don't know how. That's why I always recommended therapy. It's not just for White people, you know. And it doesn't mean you're crazy either. What makes you crazy is—and you already know—'cause I've heard you say it before," I said.

"Right. Doing the same thing over and over and expecting different results. Yeah well, back to what I was saying. After giving it a lot of thought, there are some things I can think of that I think I put at the back of my mind out of respect for you. And Mom, I gave this a lot of thought, and you know I have to be honest with you. I've not wanted to tell you this before, but as of late, I've been sitting with myself and thinking about it. Here it is…*ummm*, when we were with Stetson, to me it seems like we had a good family structure—you know it was me, you, India, and Stetson. Even though he wasn't my biological father, he always treated me like I was his son. I mean, don't get me wrong, he disciplined me…he didn't play. I got whippings and stuff like that, but I knew it was coming from a place of love. I even remember Granny Miller. She wasn't my real grandmother, and even with his entire family, they all embraced me," Zach said.

He was referring to Stetson, India's dad, and Granny Miller who was Stetson's mother. I witnessed firsthand what Zach had remembered was true. The Miller family always treated Zach like he was their own. They never once treated him any different. Even after our relationship ended, the Millers considered us their family.

I listened. I already knew where he was headed. This was a turning point for both of us. I'd longed for my son to have an authentic moment with me, and just as I knew how important it was for me to lay my cards on the table and be real with him, I knew there was no way I would be a coward and renege from having our crucial conversation at this point, by not hearing my son out.

"At that time, you know I didn't even have my own father around and truthfully, I never missed him because Stetson made sure I wasn't lacking," Zach said, and I knew what he was saying about his father, Leon, was true.

Then as he continued to verbalize the hurt from the past, he emphasized, "So, if you have to ask me, I think about all those times and how our lives shifted so drastically when y'all split up. And to make matters worse, no one ever talked to us about that situation either or what was going on between the two of you. I never saw a fight or an argument, no lead-up to him leaving. He was gone—like I mean, we didn't know if it was our fault or what was going on. Then after he left, it seemed you hadn't even given yourself air to breathe when you started seeing Radcliffe, then you married him before we could even blink. We're like what the heck's going on, and to say it was like day and night, you have no idea because most times you worked those long hours and commuted. It was pure D hell.

"There were times we would come home from school, and he'd be there with us during the in-between time, and when I tell you he did *not* treat me and India like his own. There was big-time favoritism when Shea was born. Do you remember he made us wear those masks when Shea came home from the hospital? That was just the tip of the iceberg. So, you can only imagine how I must've felt back then. All of that compounded my confusion. I was around eleven years old. I think India was six. I guess nobody ever sat down to talk to me about how I felt about any of that 'cause we were kids whose feelings and opinions didn't matter, and to my knowledge, nobody did that with India either. But you know she's a lot different than me. She speaks her mind where I just kind of…you know…keep to myself. But yeah, I was going through some misery. It was a difficult time because we had our lives completely shaken upside down. There's no other way for me to put it," Zach said, and I suppose once he got going, he decided to let it all out, so he had more to say.

"And then there were times when you and Rad were going through things, and you might not have thought that I knew you were going through those things, but I saw a lot. And I will say, I didn't like what I saw, and I wanted to do something to protect our home from him, but I was a child under him, and although he never hit me or you, it was his trifling behavior—his words were vicious and intimidating. And those things bothered me as a child. You know there were times I witnessed him being disrespectful even to you, and I wanted so bad to stand up for you, to literally beat his ass, but I knew there'd be trouble, probably more for me than him. I used to be so angry back then. I saw how hard you worked for our family, and to know that when you were away at work, you spent so many hours away from home, I'd hear him talking about you. I heard him talking about me and India. He just didn't treat us the same, Mom. Now, I will never say this to Shea because she has good memories and had great experiences with her dad. To her, he was a good father, but as far as a good stepparent to me and India, I gotta tell you, Mom, in all honesty, he was the worst. It was traumatic for me and India growing up in that house, and I'm telling you this because you've asked me, not once, not twice, but several times. And now, it's time, I've gotta come clean.

"I've given it a lot of thought. I just didn't want to say anything. Maybe I should have come to you back then. I just didn't think it was that big a deal, so I didn't say anything. I didn't want to seem like no punk—like he was right, that I was weak, but you wouldn't let up. You kept asking me if anything had happened to me. Even when I thought my life was better and that I had gotten over that stuff with Rad, you must've been able to see that something was bothering me. And I guess it's a good thing that you kept probing me over and over throughout the years, otherwise I don't believe I would've made any correlation between the past and how I react to relationships as an adult. So that's about all I can attribute it to. You know, and *ummm,* and I'm not saying, you know, he's all the blame. I'm just saying, you know, if I had to think of any type of childhood trauma that would be the one thing that blatantly comes to mind as to what could have happened to me, that right there was enough, believe me. That for me was the majority of my childhood trauma. But as far as I can remember about how you tried to raise me, India, and Shea, I think I can speak for all of us, we felt the love when you were home, but when you weren't home, it was an entirely different atmosphere. It was entirely different," Zach said as if it was painful just to relive it as he was telling me the story.

"I'm so sorry for putting you all through those times, Zach, but I'm glad for your honesty, and like I said before, I know I made a lot of mistakes. I dropped the ball. I can't undo that now. It is what it is," I managed to mouthed, barely audibly. "You know, had I been in a different mental space, I would have handled things much differently. You all were my first priority then as you are now, although my actions certainly didn't line up to show you. If you looked up young and dumb in the dictionary, I'm sure you would've seen my picture. I didn't want to be an adult at sixteen. I still wanted to hang out with my friends and do teenager like things, have fun, and so forth. I thought if I worked and provided for your basic needs that I'd fulfilled my parental duty. I didn't give you guys much in terms of emotional support—no, I didn't. The truth is, I never received much emotional support from either of my parents. Basically, I couldn't give what I knew nothing about. I'm a much different person now. I've evolved. I believe I'm emotionally mature now. And like I said before, I believe I would handle things a lot differently from how I did then. See, what I didn't know then was I simply didn't have the mental capacity to stand up for me, let alone you. Don't misunderstand me. I had been reared in a household where verbal abuse was the standard. When Granny got upset, she would cuss and fuss. My grandfather cussed and fussed, so I didn't understand the ramifications of verbal abuse because that's just the way it was. That doesn't make it right though. I know better now.

"I also know it's a lie that sticks and stones may break bones, but words will never hurt. That's not true at all. Words do hurt, and I know that now. Even though we all managed to escape physical abuse, you were abused verbally. Those words harmed you, and for that, I have much regret. I was wrong, and I'm sorry for that. So, if you will accept what I'm telling you, I hope that we can move forward and *ummm* try to heal from that. I intend to have the same conversation with India. The last thing I want is for any of you to carry some sort of adverse childhood trauma, be it physical or mental or whatever without acknowledging it. I don't want to act like it doesn't exist as if there's nothing there when there is," I said.

"Yeah, adverse childhood trauma ain't no joke, is it, Mom?" Zach said.

"No, it's not. It's a real thing. And I also want to say, you know, you might even want to consider getting your own therapist. You unpacked quite a bit. Hopefully, you feel somewhat relieved to have that weight lifted. Know this: I'm your mother and your number one advocate, but I'm not a therapist. I can only put in the work for myself. I can't be your therapist and mine too. I'm still a work in progress myself, you know what I'm saying? But honey, I love you with everything in me, and just know that I'm here for you. I can't stress that enough."

"I know that, Mom. India and Shea know that too. Yeah, we all know that. We don't have any doubt about that, and we're going to be okay."

I felt good about my conversation with Zach, even though he really let me have it, respectfully so, and in the end, I felt that talk was a much-needed thing for us to have. And overall, I accepted it as a win and an opportunity to give myself more grace and a chance for us to move forward and continue to grow as a family. I found it funny—ironic rather—how in my life, I had been having some of the same thoughts over and over and over regarding shame, embarrassment, and *blah, blah, blah,* and not once did I give it a thought that it might be me that needed to not only shift my thought pattern, but I needed to change some behavior patterns.

I had been spinning my wheels trying to fix other people, specifically the ones nearest and dearest to my heart, specifically my children. I had been so busy trying to make them meet my unrealistic standards, wanting them to fit some artificial mold, along with placing an unachievable high bar in an attempt to make them reach my goals rather than hearing, seeing, and loving them right where there were. I refused to let this be a proverbial wall between us, nor would this be an impasse to our overall well-being. I consciously decided this too shall pass but would require much work.

I shifted from side to side in my bed, flipping my pillow over to its cooler side as I kicked my leg from beneath the down covers. Would I ever get to sleep? I gave up and lay there face up in the pitch darkness thinking and recapping all of what was said during our conversation. When out of nowhere, I thought, *Damn, I forgot to ask Zach about that alleged baby daddy situation.* I shrugged it off, closed my eyes, and hoped that I'd drift off to sleep. The last thing I remember thinking was *I guess that's a topic for another time. Zach's a grown man. That's his issue. I'm sure he'll let me know how it turned out when he's ready. I'm going to leave that alone for now. Right now, we have bigger fish to fry. I hope tomorrow is a better day.*

CHAPTER 23

I was still trying to sort out my conversation with Zach. I knew I needed to speak with India and Shea while I was still in my zone of courage. I was hard pressed to have the same discussion with my girls. I didn't know how I would go about it, but what I did know was it was going to get done.

Zach got with me later in the week and said that he had talked with his alleged baby mama, the girl who had reached out to him with the claim that he'd fathered her child. Zach said he had agreed to a DNA test, and as soon as he received the results, he would let me know. I was glad to know that Zach was being accountable to that situation and handling his business.

Shea reached out and told me that she decided that she and Corliss were not going to move in together. She said, after giving it more thought and looking at the pros and cons, they both decided to give each other time to grow individually before moving in together. Shea said she felt it was better that way, and she confessed she didn't know if she was ready for a live-in girlfriend yet.

I guess this was the week for reach out and touch. I even received a text from my granddaughter Zora, and she wasn't asking for a Zelle, CashApp, or Apple Pay, which pleasantly surprised me. I read the excitement in her text, which was rather lengthy. In fact, it was a group text to all of us—her mom India, Shea, Zach, and me. Zora's message shared the news about a new business venture called a product influencer. She said she had reached ninety-eight thousand followers and was thrilled about it. No one in our group asked her how much money she was making or how follower count equated to income, but I for one was praying it was enough to sustain her life, and if I had to assume, judging from the replies and cash emojis in our family group chat, Zora was making money.

I still had my doubts though, and before I could even ask, Zora also shared in the chat that being a social influencer led to the potential to make a lot of money and earn a living just by, as the name itself implies, influencing other people to buy products and brands.

I had to admit, I didn't really buy into the whole idea at first, but I didn't want to be a Debbie downer or a dream killer, so of course, Zora being my one and only grandchild, I supported her desires and wished her much success. Besides, as I thought about it, Zora had said she had been playing around with the whole idea since the shutdown, and I wasn't oblivious to how creative the world had become in terms of using social media as a way to bring in multiple streams of income. I'd heard folks talk about it on *The*

Ellen DeGeneres Show, The Real, and other talk shows. And I knew anything was possible once a person put their mind to what they wanted and if they wanted it bad enough.

Zora said she'd been surprised at how well things picked up and how she had been making hella money. And according to India, Zora was right. Her business venture had paid off. As India always did, she co-signed what Zora was telling us in the chat and went as far as to say since she'd last checked, Zora's IG account, her numbers had soared and come to find out, Zora's followers had grown to over two hundred thousand followers versus how many Zora thought she had a while ago. I still couldn't imagine how that equated to dollars, but if it was the follower count, then I sure hoped that meant that my granddaughter's financial status grew exponentially as well.

It sounded interesting to me, so like I said, I suppose it's a good thing, so whatever works for them, that's fine by me as long as it's legal and safe. I'm learning to stay in my lane and mind the business that pays me. Also in the chat, India nonchalantly dropped the news that she and Malcolm had decided to tie the knot, and they were planning to have a private ceremony and maybe do something like a large reception at a later date. In her words, when the world opened up again. Everyone in the chat responded with heart emojis and congratulatory responses, so that was another something we all agreed with and were happy about. So, to say all was well with the family for the most part was a win for this group chat.

I hadn't received the typical sidebar text rolling eyes or confused emoji from neither Zach or Shea when Zora or India spoke, so that was a sign that we were all in unison. Sometimes the same sidebar text came from India about something Zach or Shea said. I was always the middleman. Who knows, they all probably did the same about me when I said something they viewed as outlandish, so whatever. All of them knew not to say anything disrespectful to my face.

From the outside looking in at other families, I thought most everyone else was normal but me and my family—they were damn near perfect, and we weren't. I couldn't have been any further from the truth. There's no such thing as a perfect family, not even close, whatever that means. I, for one, wanted to believe there'd be less strife between siblings who lived in two-parent homes and birthed by the same mother and father. I don't know where I got that fallacy from because hearing stories about some of my relatives, friends, and other acquaintances, my perception of the so-called normal perfect family structure did not exist. But I've since learned even in two-parent households there can be just as much dysfunctional in families than if there were a single parent with children and different fathers. It took me many years to see that as the truth. It just is, and I've learned better. If anybody tries to tell me different, they're lying. I've seen *whole* biological brothers and sisters going at it with each other sometimes worse than half-siblings did with one another. Everyone has their own set of home issues—be it generational, immature emotional parenting issues, abuse, or whatever, there is always something. The difference is knowing how to heal from it so we're not repeating the same vicious cycles over and over.

Something about hearing Maysa's story resonated with me. And I think it finally hit home for me that what it looks like on the outside is not what it is. Growing up as a child, my mother Bea would tell me things about other families, and I'd always heard such was the case, but it hits differently when someone decides to trust me enough to share their story with me. It was like the saying goes, *straight from the horse's mouth.* Well, when someone tells me something firsthand, that lets me know other folks have issues same as me and sometimes on a deeper level.

Several weeks passed before I heard from Maysa again. I had made my mind up to give her some space to breathe, and I was relieved to hear from her when I did. I was more than happy to hear that Maysa's tone hadn't seemed as devastating as the last time we'd talked, and gathering from how the call was going, I felt things must've gotten better.

"You sound good, friend," I said.

"Yeah, girl. Sorry I haven't called or texted you before now. I've been so busy. It was really touch and go with Momma and trying to keep the business—or what's left of my business—going and Olivia straight. Well…it's just been a lot to deal with. But we're all doing much better now. As I recall, the last time we talked, I told you about my horrible situation with my brother, so let me jump right into to how things are going. How about that miserable bastard ended up having a near fatal accident on the railroad? Long story short, he must've had a vision from the Lord Himself 'cause he sent word by my uncle—you remember the one I told you about who always handled things for me whenever there was trouble to be handled in our family? Anyway, my uncle assured me again. Girl, I don't have to worry about my brother ever coming near me, Momma, Olivia, or none of that," Maysa said with victory in her voice.

"Really?" I said, curious to know more.

"Yeah. So, I decided not to press charges against his ass. But I did sit Olivia down and had a very long talk with her and told her everything. I just didn't want to live with that burden any longer. I refuse to give that monster any more power over my life," Maysa said solemnly.

"Wow, that took a lot of courage, Maysa. I'm proud of you for doing that. And you're right, you took your power back. So, how did Olivia take everything you told her?" I cautiously probed my friend.

"Well, it was tough at first. It really was. I'll just say this: We're working our way through it. Like I said before, Momma did what she believed was right for our family at that time by not outing him, but that wasn't enough to protect me. Once Olivia understood my intentions, that I was trying to protect her and be there for her, and not lie to her, I think she got it. I want her to know there is nothing too big or too small that she can't feel safe to come to me about," Maysa said.

"Well, that's good to hear," I said.

"The other thing is I've decided to get Olivia a therapist. I've seen someone in the past along with talking to our pastor, but I need to get back on a regular mental health schedule too. I had so much bottled up in me that it was hard for me to process how I was really feeling about things that happened to me in my past. It's going to be a journey, but I'm ready to put in the work," Maysa said.

"You're so right. It is a journey worth going on because, take it from me, you're worth it. You owe it to yourself to put your self-care first. You've only got one you and one shot at this thing called life. When it's over, it's a wrap. So be the best you now, while you can. Do what you need to do to see to that," I said reassuringly to my friend.

I was elated to hear Maysa's news, and I was glad to hear that she and Olivia were getting therapy. Looking back, I didn't know when it had exactly changed, but the dynamics seemed to have deviated in the relationship between Fav and me. All I know is sometime during the shutdown we had been conversing more, checking in on each other, and we had become more like close acquaintances, but then as I thought about it, that had always been part of my nature, being kind, caring, and nurturing to people I cared about. That was a characteristic that had always been easy for me. And knowing the type of guy Fav was, he'd always been a loving person who I'd always known to be an equally kind-hearted person whenever I was in his presence. Even though over the years, we'd been in such an erratic sensual involvement, it wasn't his personality but the inconsistency of his behavior though that had been my angst with him. But now, since I didn't require anything from him in terms of time and commitment such as what occurs in an amorous relationship, I took hearing from him as nonchalantly as it came. I don't know, maybe that was my wall of protection.

At any rate, I had evolved. I felt it internally. Gone were the heartthrobs and longing to be with him. I still desired for sensuality with a man, but I wasn't merely fixated on just that anymore. There was much more to my life than that. I realized I wanted something on a deeper connection with someone. I was already more than enough. I was deserving, sincere, established, and I knew I possessed all the qualities to compliment the best of any compatible man available. I didn't know if I'd ever meet my Prince Charming or not, but I knew my life would go on with or without him. I am confident, I know my worth, and I know what I want, and I am unwilling to settle for anything less than what I want.

CHAPTER 24

Spring of 2021, Maysa and I met for breakfast one morning, and afterward, I followed her to the Range Rover dealership where she had to drop her car off for service, then as planned, we had a much-needed girls' day as some of the nail spas and hair salons were reopening. And since Maysa already had the day off, we decided to go and have our nails and feet done. We didn't go anywhere publicly without masks. Still, it was nice to be able to get somewhat back to how things were prior to the shutdown. Afterward, we both decided to head on out to Fair Park so Maysa could get her first COVID-19 vaccination.

It had been a year now, and we were still doing church virtually, and slowly but surely, the malls and other things of that nature had started to reopen as well as most restaurants—at least the ones that hadn't gone out of business due to the shutdown. Life was different, but it was manageable. Small groups of friends and family had created what was called COVID-19 bubbles, which was where small groups of relatives or friends decided to band together to coexist during the post pandemic by limiting the number of people we interacted with on a regular basis to keep the spread of COVID-19 down. I was part of Maysa and her family's COVID-19 bubble, which was one way we were able to manage during the pandemic.

Most times, I kept to myself. Thanks to virtual communication, I remained in touch with my children, other close friends, relatives, and of course Fav. The children and I had weekly phone chats, either via text or virtual face-to-face chats. Life was as good as we could reasonably achieve. Zach seemed to be better mentally and even reached out to tell me he'd received the results from the completed a DNA, which had returned negative. Zach wasn't the child's father. I could hear the disappointment in his voice as he spoke.

"So, you don't sound happy. Tell me how you're feeling," I said to Zach.

"I've always wanted to be a father. I think that was a bit of a void in my life. Seemed like most of the fellas in my circle have kids already, and sometimes the fellas can be hard toward guys like me who don't have any children. You wouldn't know anything about that, Mom, 'cause you're a woman, but I hear I'm shooting blanks and stuff like that. Yeah, I'd laugh it off, but those words hurt. I just never let on how those things affected me, so to answer your question, I guess I don't know how I'm feeling. In some ways, I'm hurt. In some ways, I feel inadequate, you know, like I'm less than a man. And in some ways, I'm triggered back to those feelings of intimidation I used to get from Rad, how I used to feel so incapable. I just can't describe it," Zach said, and I could hear the hurt in his voice.

I was triggered to want to fix it for him, to remove his pain, but at the same time, I had to remind myself to sit back and allow him the chance to go through what he needed to go through to heal. I was proud of him for having the courage to finally share his emotions with me.

"Remember when I kept asking you if you had been molested, and you kept saying no? Finally, you let down your guard and shared with me how you felt about the things you went through with Rad..." I cautiously tried to choose my words with Zach as I spoke.

"Yeah, and I told you that wasn't the case with me. I wasn't molested," Zach said.

"Yes. I believe you. All I want to say is verbal abuse and emotional trauma can be just as bad as sexual abuse. Verbal abuse stays with you. Whoever said sticks and stones hurt and words never do was telling a lie 'cause words sting like a bee, and bee stings hurt like hell and can kill you if left untreated. The point I'm trying to make is—and I know I've said more than once—but it's 'cause I really think you should consider it—" I carefully said and was cut off before I finished.

"Therapy. Yeah, I've thought about it. It just seems so corny though, and I'm not sure where I should start. It seems every time I drink, my life worsens. I mean, I like kicking it and having a good time, but I don't seem to know when to quit. I keep going to the point where I intentionally provoke others to verbal fights. I mean it gets so bad until it leads to me saying some terrible things to people I really care about. I know it isn't called for, but I find myself doing and feeling so bad afterward. That's when I know I've crossed the line, but then it's too late, and Mom, I don't blame you for anything either. You did a good job with all of us. We had a good life—well, for the most part—and I know that firsthand. I have had more than a few of my homies tell me the same thing, that they look at our family and think how good we had it when they didn't have it as good as we did. This is just me. I can't even blame any one particular person for me or my actions. I do take ownership for my behavior. I just don't know how to change it. I know most of the time you guys don't believe I feel bad about my negative behavior but I do."

"Yeah, well sounds like you have identified one thing. You do know alcoholism runs in our family, right? My grandfather, my mother—your grandmother—they were undiagnosed alcoholics. You see, alcoholism is nothing to play with. More important than that, they say alcohol gives a person the courage to say and do what's already in them to do and speak, and if that's true, you've already identified some triggers that take you to the point of no return. Sounds to me what's left is for you to learn how to manage those triggers so that when they come about, you have the tools you need to work through them and not take you to that over-the-edge point. Believe me, a good therapist will work with you to process those things and will help you heal through that. Therapy gave me what I needed to live better and to manage my own childhood trauma. I believe it can do the same thing for you. Think about it and give it a shot before you rule it out completely," I said.

"I'll look into it," Zach said.

To me, Zach showed his growth. It was these types of conversations that I cherished having with my son. I wanted him to know he had a safe place to share his feelings without criticism from me or me guilt tripping him for making certain choices in life. I have grown to realize it's hard enough for any of us who have made mistakes to have to deal with the consequences without having to hear "I told you so" from anyone else for that matter.

As far as I was concerned, I saw all the signs of growth myself for that matter. I was no longer about trying to control every aspect of my adult children's lives. After having had a similar chat with India and Shea about the past and how I felt I had dropped the ball, I realized that no matter what happened then, I could not go through life carrying guilt, regret, and past hurt. At this point, I was only responsible for how I moved going forward. The reality was it is what it is. I could not be responsible for how they processed the things they went through. I am human, and I have made mistakes and will likely make more. That's the nature of the beast. And like I reiterated to Zach, I verbalized the same message to India and Shea.

And now that the white elephant had been cleared out the room, we now have safe space to address our family concerns openly and honestly. I know there's going to be times, when things will occur that we'll disagree and not see eye to eye on, but as long as we respect one another's individual terms and boundaries, I'm hopeful we can move toward our healing journey together as one big happy but imperfect family. At the end of the day—and at the beginning too—that's pretty much all I ask for.

CHAPTER 25

I didn't see it coming, but during the pandemic, my relationship with Fav changed. The nature of our conversations and the frequency in which we spoke with one another had come a long way. Before the shutdown and over the course of time, whenever Maysa or one of my other girlfriends would ask me whether I'd heard from Fav, I playfully dubbed him as my pen pal given that much of our interaction had been through texts, though that's not the case anymore. Maysa was perplexed by our dynamics, and she expressed her confusion openly. None of my girlfriends truly grasped it, and that's precisely why I avoided delving into the subject of him. It was a touchy topic that, for me, crossed the line.

This new thing between me and Fav sort of caught me off guard too. For so many years, I'd been conditioned to not expect his calls or texts as often because that was how things had been between us. I believe that was my way of shielding myself from hurt and disappointment. And to add to my wall of defense, I created a mindset of you don't call me, I don't call you; you stop calling me, I stop expecting it. My adverse childhood experiences had taught me that behavior too. To think, I could have saved myself all that time and anguish had I known how to communicate what I wanted instead of playing emotional roulette with my true feelings. But nooo, not me, Bria Twon. I was too prideful to let any man into my heart. I didn't want to be hurt or made a fool of.

And I carried that behavior over into my adult interactions in relationships. I wasn't a good communicator. I thought I was, but essentially, I avoided conflict, I avoided having difficult conversations. I knew how to end a relationship that I felt no longer made me comfortable, but I wasn't good at doing the work it took to resolve one. I'd plan my exit strategy and leave before I'd attempt to work things out. I knew I had that technique down pat. But that was then. Now I'm a different person. I felt safe, confident, and damn sure of who and what I wanted, so fast forward to the person I am today. I am no longer fearful of speaking up for myself before I reach my boiling point as that also was something I had learned about me. I went into defense mode when something was out of sync with my emotional state, which most times seemed to be erratic of me.

I didn't have any issues being shut down at home during the national shutdown. Home was my happy place. I knew full well how to entertain myself. I suppose that, too, was something I had been conditioned to do as a child that had carried over into my adulthood. And the more I talked with Fav, I learned we had shared a lot of the same traits.

"Hey, baby." After all this time, just the sound of Fav's voice still had a way of sending heat through my body. He made everything sound so sensual naturally.

"Hey, baby. How are you?" I replied.

"I'm missing you," he said.

"I miss you too," I said, trying not to sound too corny.

"I hear the airlines are back up. They are filling every other seat, with the requirement to wear a mask in the airports and on the plane, so what do you think, we give it a try and plan something?" Fav said.

"Yeah. I've been hearing that on the news as well. And sure, I'm willing to give it a try. I'm all vaxed up, and from what you've told me, so are you. What'd you have in mind?" I asked.

I thought he'd never ask. I was so ready for him until I couldn't see straight. Fav never not once didn't turn me on. Even when I hoped it wouldn't be good, it was better than good in his arms. The warmth of his muscular body was sensational.

"Cool," he said.

And just like that, every other weekend, it was either my place or his. Our frequent flyer miles were adding up very quickly. I smiled as I reminisced about one of our discussions as we lay next to each other. Fav had said, "Baby, I wasn't good at vocalizing how I felt, and I know now that left you filled with so much uncertainty about us. I did what I had the capacity to do at that time to show you how much I loved you, but you didn't seem to grasp it. I mean, I know there were times I didn't make the time to have the important conversations with you, and yes, that was my bad. I take ownership for that, but damn, didn't the things I would do show you something?"

"No, they didn't. I knew how I felt when we were together. And yes, I put up a façade like I wasn't bothered. I mean you're an intelligent man. You operated a Fortune 500 company. I shouldn't have had to completely spell it out for you, and since you didn't tell me anything substantial about us. I didn't want to assume, so I moved accordingly."

"Wow. It just goes to show what a little communication means in a relationship. As a man, I thought we were secure because I knew how I felt, but what I failed to do was tell you those things. You won't have that to be unclear about any longer. I will shout it to the rooftops; in the middle of the street; on a plane, bus, or from a bicycle. I'll put it on social media, and you know I'm not a social media type. Anything. I will do anything to let you know what you mean to me. Look in my eyes, baby. I mean every word," Fav softly spoke, and from the glazed look in his eyes, I felt his sincerity.

I was almost inclined to look away—again. I was hit with my old behavior to run, hide from someone confronting me with a resolution. I wanted to be different from what I had been conditioned to, so instead of following my instinct to run, I looked at Fav dead in his eyes, and at that very moment, I felt so vulnerable and safe when I said to him, "I have loved you for so long."

There, I said it, and I couldn't take it back, I felt what he felt, and trusted that our hearts were in unison. I knew in that moment beyond any stretch of my imagination that what I'd been feeling about him, that Fav felt the same for me. And it felt good, real good to know what we'd shared hadn't been some casual affair as if two insatiable lovers lusting after one another in vain. This was our season. We'd been prepared for this time. Our respecting the process had proven to exceed any of our expectations to what having and building a profound love shared by two could be. We leaned toward one another to kiss. I felt his moist lips lightly pecking my forehead, then my nose, then our lips met in an affectionate kiss. Afterward, we embraced, and I felt the wetness from his eyes on my back, and my joyful tears faded into his muscular chest. I breathed a sigh of relief. This was a new chapter for us. Like a ship left ashore, our love had been patiently waiting on our acknowledgement, and like the quote, "Ships are made for the sea, just as love is made for the soul," I understood the assignment, we were made for this.

EPILOGUE

November 2024

I had been so focused on checking off every box on my list, and it seemed that as soon as I looked up, just like that I was sixty-two, and I wondered where all the time had gone. Suddenly, I realized how I had spent a large majority of my life. I was that person. I had prepared for the next accomplishment after the next. And never once had I known I was already reaping the benefit of one of my preconceived ideas of what I wanted next. I hadn't learned how to celebrate my wins, let alone how to embrace where I was now.

Even the times I was posed with the thought of what I would say to my younger self, I had no idea what I would say, what advice I would give me, what encouragement I could add, or what I would applaud. Now, as time went on and looking back at things in my life, I have a self-awareness of how I have had so many missed opportunities to give myself grace. And of how many times I had missed telling myself that I was enough, that "hey, girl. It's okay. You messed up that time, but you get another chance. You got this. It's okay. You can do this, and guess what? You did it." I had lost touch with the reality of being because I was so busy looking at a preconceived notion of what could've, would've, should've happened.

There were too many tomorrows in my life. It was now time for me to press pause and take a breather. Hypothetically, I heard the voice of India who would often say to me, "Mom, it's okay to relax and do nothing" because she knew as well as I knew that I found it hard to just do nothing and to breathe. For whatever reason, I felt guilty whenever I wasn't active. Then again, there were times I was busy doing nothing, not actually being productive and getting things done. But one thing the pandemic taught me by default was it was okay to sit still because I had no choice but to sit still with my own thoughts and to take solace in there is joy and pain in this life, and that's just the reality of it all. Nothing is perfect. Family's not perfect, and there's no such thing as normal. We all have some sort of dysfunction in our lives, and to accept that is normal per se.

Life is filled with changes and turn-arounds. I have now learned to take life as it comes and to embrace one day at a time to understand where I am. There is nothing more soothing than to be present in the moment and to let the past be the past. The present is called the present for a reason—it is a gift, a present, and what better gift than the moment I'm in than right now.

Years ago, I wasn't ready for this time. Life has taught me so much, and I'm grateful for everything I've ever gone through. I'm happy for my journey and have come to realize that I wouldn't be who I am without every obstacle I've ever faced. All those things from my past helped shape me into the person I am today. Yes, it was a challenge for me to get it, I mean for me to accept my reality. I could either cling to the pain and let it hinder my growth or use it as lessons from each experience.

I used to grimace at the thought of confrontation. I didn't know how to have hard conversations. I didn't know how to forgive myself for my past failures, but one thing is for sure, I know better, and I know my worth.

Thank God I had the courage to put in the work toward healing. Otherwise, I would have missed this moment. I was presenting a healthier me to a good relationship. I was a mess. It took me all this time to get it—to really get it—and I have no regrets. Had I not gone through all of what I had, I would not be the person I am today. I cherish my relationships with my children. No, we are not perfect, and I am not striving to be. I am grateful that we have a mutual love for one another and are here for one another. When they were younger, I held their hands. Now that they are older, I have their backs. We have boundaries for one another, and we respect those boundaries. We are all a work in progress. I have learned to breathe, exhale, live, and let live.

"I'm glad you are happy, Mom—I mean really happy. I see it in your eyes, and your skin even has a bronzy glow. I like that in you," India said as she was putting the final touches on my makeup.

"Well, thank you for noticing. And I you know what? I am happy. But you know what, more than that I am at peace and filled with joy, and that's something that can't be taken away. It's almost unexplainable," I said.

"Yeah, well we can all see it. Zach, Shea, and Zora even said as much. And just in case no one has told you lately, we're proud of you and glad you're our mother. We wish you and Beau—'cause *ummm,* no ma'am, we refuse to call him Fav," India jokingly said as she snapped her fingers in the air and jerked her head to demonstrate she meant it, then she got serious and said, "all the happiness in the world. You both deserve it," India said then she tenderly cradled my face with her hands and kissed me on my cheek.

"Girl, stop now. You know I can't cry. I'll have these lashes crossways before this ceremony begins, and you know we can't go out like that now, girl. So cut that out," I said, trying to deflect from the moment.

I still couldn't believe we had managed to get the entire family to South Africa for our wedding ceremony. That took some bending of arms in itself. But my Fav had insisted on seeing to it that all of my children were there. I was more than surprised when Malcolm came, along with Maysa, Harmony, Connie, and Suni. And there were a few of Fav's relatives there as well. It all felt like a dream.

"Nah, you'll be alright, Momma-girl. I got you. Those lashes ain't going nowhere tuh-day," India jokingly said.

"Girl, it's just like you to have a fairy tale–ass wedding in South Africa of all damn places in the world. And who but you could pull it off to have all of us here again?" Suni asked in her bodacious voice as only she could speak.

"Yeah, girl, you're going to have to get ready. Everyone is waiting on you," Harmony said.

"Well, looks like she's ready, so what are we all waiting for?" India said. Her makeup was done, and we could come in the room.

"Bria, are you okay? Say something. You're starting to scare me. You look like you're in a trance. Are you having second thoughts?" Connie probed, staring at me in bewilderment like she'd seen a ghost.

"I know damn well she'd better not be getting no cold feet. Not now, not after all the money we done spent to get here and this tight-ass shapewear I'm wearing," Suni said.

"Suni, come on now. She's not getting cold feet, and please tone it down a little. You're making me nervous, and it's not even my damn wedding," Harmony said to Suni in a chastising voice before she directed her concern back toward me.

"Girl, what's wrong? Bri, are you okay?" Harmony rushed nearer to me, and like clockwork, Connie and Suni followed her lead.

I looked up at each one of my girlfriends one by one, sizing them up individually. I was lost in deep introspection. Just that quick, I saw flashbacks from the past, as if my whole life had been rewound and shown on a big screen right before my eyes. I saw my childhood, instances with my mother Bea, my past relationships, moments with my children, and memorable things I had gone through with each of my girlfriends. And here we were as if someone hit a fast forward in time. I conscientiously had to suppress my instinct to either fight or flee. When I heard a voice succinctly, it conveyed all the assurance I needed with these few words, "Yes, you deserve to be here. Yes, you deserve to be loved. Yes, you are lovable. Yes, you have been prepared for this."

I felt emboldened by that message. I was ready for love, to give love and receive love. Most importantly, I wanted my girlfriends to know how much I appreciated their unwavering sisterhood. A sisterhood that was chosen and had been more than a mere friendship. We had gone through so much together, and I wanted to verbally let them know how much they meant to me. But my brain's signal to my lips wasn't registering anything, and all I could manage to say was nothing. All I had was a look that *said* it all, and before I could gather my thoughts, the look from each of them was mutual. We all flung into a group hug for what seemed like infinity until we heard a knock at the door.

"Showtime, ladies. It's time." It was Maysa. I had asked her to be my bridal assistant to keep us on track.

"Okay, girls. Let's get this going. I love you all so much, and thank you," I finally managed to verbalize.

"Okay, knock it off with all this mushy shit," Suni said to break the ice.

Like a group of school-aged girls caught talking and snickering in church by their Sunday school teacher, we all burst out laughing through misty eyes. Then it was as if everything was back to normal as we released ourselves, straightened our attire and regained our composure before each lady headed out the door one by one in the formation they were assigned for the wedding processional with me remaining as the last one to exit the room along with Maysa who had a once-over glimpse of me to ensure everything was intact.

I wasn't easily impressed by grandiose gestures, but Fav took my breath away when he flew into Dallas and got down on one knee. I vividly remembered that day. Almost immediately, when I'd opened my front door, he was there. Fav pulled out the biggest diamond I'd ever laid eyes on, and he asked me to do life with him. He said he couldn't imagine living without me and shared with me that the one thing the pandemic had taught him was being apart from me was something he didn't want to experience again in his lifetime. I could see the tears in his eyes as he professed his love for me.

Never would I have imagined that Fav and I could have come full circle. My mom had always said no man is going to marry a woman if he can get the milk for free. I had no intentions on marrying again, so it had never occurred to me not to think anything was wrong with the nature of how things had been with our relationship. Nor had I believed I would ever have needed to change my course of direction of how I'd been going about doing anything in that regard. Then suddenly, I got this proverbial epiphany—my "aha" moment occurred—and I'll admit, I could no longer deny what I'd known for years. I had been misleading myself. It began to faze me that my life, like a navigation system, was filled with unexpectant twists and turns, and it was time to change my course of direction.

In the grand scheme of life, haste makes waste. I can't say enough about respecting the process. No, I didn't become all righteous and stuff, and I was still fine with getting my intimate desires met by the one man who turned me on the most. With Fav, I knew it was unequivocally reciprocal and mutual. Yes, that had been my choice, but also my choice was I knew I wasn't going to sit on the sidelines and wait for things to change nor did I plan on doing that sort of thing forever, nor did I want to be an old senior citizen sidepiece. So, when Fav hit me with the "baby, please" after I'd said I had to give us some thought, I could no longer resist his proposal when his eyes met mine and he said, "I want to do life with you." I knew he meant it. I felt it in the depths of my soul.

I said yes, and he crossed my threshold and swept me up into his muscular caramel-toned arms. We embraced in my doorway, kissing and caressing each other like two sick lovebirds. We were pulling at each other's clothes trying to touch skin when we both caught ourselves midstream and realized the door was still ajar. It was magical. I'd known for so long how much I loved him, but I had no idea how he felt. All along, I had been too full of pride to have admitted my true feelings for him. And ditto for him. It seemed we had a lot in common in that regard. Over the course of time, we had become the best of friends. He had become comfortable enough with me and expressed how he had been self-absorbed and overambitious during his career over the years and had experienced commitment issues because his childhood sweetheart whom he had married right after college had cheated on him with one of his frat brothers.

Our love had been a slow burn for many years. It is not often that a love like ours worked. I wanted to pinch myself. I thought I had drifted off to sleep, but this time it was no dream. This was real. I am glad I didn't miss out on my now. I remember hearing somewhere that sometimes we get so caught up in what's next that we miss our opportunities to embrace the right now. I felt like Fav was my one true love. God had prepared me for him, and I was ready to love him unconditionally. In everything I'd ever gone through, I had been groomed for him. Waiting for him had been my greatest gift from God. The precious gift of delayed gratification had been well worth the wait.

And the best part about it was I felt the love reciprocated. I didn't need him, I wanted him. He completed me because he added to me. His love made me want to be a better version of myself. He was the up to my down, he was my person, and I was his. We played footsies together like two young lovers. Feeling the warmth of our skin against each other's and giggling as we nibbled at each other's lips while entangled in each other's arms was exhilarating and something we'd both longed for. We whispered through stolen kisses, we shared ideas of planting a garden together, fishing, chilling on the patio—all the things old, retired people do, like looking for our glasses when they were already on our faces and searching for our telephones when we were talking on them—and we planned to do all those things together for infinity.

Fav and I wed at Memoire Wedding Venue in Muldersdrift, South Africa, in an intimate setting with a mountainous backdrop, vast skies, trees, and nature. In the distance were the sounds of cicadas and croaking frogs. We wanted a once-in-a-lifetime love inspired by us, a once-in-a-lifetime love for each other. Our wedding venue was filled with beautiful opulent white floral arrangements accented with white-and-gold trimmed satin, linen, and elegance. Oversized ceramic vases encased circular waterfalls on the patio, which gave off just the right element for a peaceful and magical evening.

"Let's make this a night to remember, baby," Fav whispered in my ear as he held me in his arms while we danced in the middle of our venue's dance floor.

"You already have, baby. This has been a wonderful night and a beautiful beginning of the rest of our lives. I love you, Beaumont Jackson," I whispered back in my man's ear.

"I love you, Sabria Twon—oh, my bad, Mrs. Sabria Jackson." We kissed like we'd never kissed before, like no one was watching. And we remained enmeshed in each other's arms to show our family, friends, and the world our love is a marathon and not a sprint.

Acknowledgements

To God, my heart is grateful for all things—I could write an entire book on gratefulness.

To my readers I hope this book resonates with you and holds your attention. I write for those, like me, who love fiction and seek an occasional escape from life's realities relishing in a good read with a favorite beverage. After all, reading is sexy you know!

Thank you to my family for encouraging me to pursue my dream. Special gratitude to my editor and friend, Chandra Sparks Splond, for challenging me to write like a pro and believing in me from day one. I appreciate your expertise and for accepting my project for the third time.

A heartfelt thanks to my sister circle of friends, especially Hope Montgomery, Mary Barnett, and Pat Johnson for their unwavering support. Your words of encouragement meant the world to me during moments of self-doubt. Thank you Sherry Tate for our insightful conversations about navigating life while raising young men without present fathers. Debra DeWalt and Renade Cossey, your support and prayers were my pillars when I felt inadequate. To my baby cousin, Lisa Seward, your endurance, and strength pushed me to live boldly.

To my children—Demond, Paris, and Jasmine—I thank God for blessing me with all of you, as well as my grandchildren. Paris, my real-life alter ego, your humor, and stories inspired characters in this book, bringing fictional lives to vivid perspectives. I admire your candor, strength, and wisdom. I thank you all for whatever contribution, big and small, you made to help this project come to life. And no, Paris, I won't be paying you any residuals.

ABOUT THE AUTHOR

Born and raised in Rockford, Illinois, Eartha Gatlin is the talented author behind two captivating books--The Chronicles of Bria Twon and Hey You, What About Me, Bria? Notably, her latest work, the third installment in the Bria Twon series, marks Eartha's continued exploration of fiction. As a leader and mentor, Eartha crafts relatable-situational woman's fiction with the aim of inspiring women to embrace their best selves. Through her writing, she humorously engages readers, inviting them to see aspects of themselves through the lens of her compelling characters.

Beyond her role as an author, Eartha is the proud owner of Ahtrae Publishing, LLC, where she has successfully self-published five books, including notable works like Conflict of Intere$t and No Hope by author Tyress Cunningham. Currently residing in the dynamic DFW Metroplex, Eartha Gatlin continues to contribute her unique voice and perspective to the literary world.

Stay connected with Eartha Gatlin on Instagram, Facebook, Twitter, LinkedIn, and Threads, @Author_EarthaGatlin

Printed in the USA
CPSIA information can be obtained
at www.ICGtesting.com
JSHW022103261223
54265JS00006B/31